She leaned down and reached one hand out to him, and with a glance at me, he took her hand. Pleased that he hadn't turned away as I had expected, I said, "It's okay, Sam. She's a nice lady."

Silly, inane words, but he appeared to understand. And when she went on to pick him up, he offered no resistance.

Smiling, I went back into the bedroom where we had slept. I picked up the cookie crumbs, putting them in my pocket for lack of a better place. Then I smoothed the covers and lifted the backpack. Then just as I was settling it comfortably in place, I heard the loud and ominous click once more. Whirling around, I went to the door and pushed, but it wouldn't open. I turned the knob frantically.

Nothing. I was locked in!

WITH LOVE, FROM SAM AND ME

Nadine Roberts

FAWCETT JUNIPER • NEW YORK

RLI: $\dfrac{\text{VL 6 \& up}}{\text{IL 9 \& up}}$

A Fawcett Juniper Book
Published by Ballantine Books
Copyright © 1990 by Nadine Roberts

Library of Congress Catalog Card Number: 89-91547

ISBN 0-449-70368-1

Manufactured in the United States of America

First Edition: April 1990

Prologue

IF I HAD known ahead of time that August seventeenth had the makings of the beginning of a better life for Sam and me, I would have handled everything differently. I didn't have a clue though. As far as the available evidence went, it was just another miserable steamy summer day that I would spend running after Sam and trying with even less success to keep Uncle Ed and Aunt Bonnie off my back.

There was little chance. No matter what I did, it wasn't quite what they'd had in mind. When I cleaned the house, it either took me too long or I was being "prissy." When I cooked supper, it was guaranteed to be underdone, overdone, or too early because they'd planned on having just a couple more beers before they ate.

They did have a point there. I liked to start supper as early as I could, because Uncle Ed and Aunt Bonnie nearly always hit the sack right after they ate. Then, except for the snoring, Sam and I wouldn't be bothered till morning. That's the one good thing I could say about beer: six or eight apiece, and they were out.

The day turned out a little out of the ordinary though, because two important things happened on the seventeenth of August. There was a sale on beer that Uncle Ed and Aunt Bonnie didn't know about, so I used the money I saved to mail an envelope to New York City. That was one thing. The other thing was that I kidnapped Sam and ran away from

1

home with him that night after Uncle Ed and Aunt Bonnie went to sleep.

If I had known how the first thing would turn out, I wouldn't have done the second thing. But I didn't know it. This is how it happened. Feel free to follow along if you like. It's not all bad, but I warn you, it isn't going to be an altogether pleasant journey either.

Chapter One

MY EYES WERE stinging from the sweat, and I'd just wiped the dishwater off my hands so I could wash my face and cool off a little, when I heard Aunt Bonnie's familiar screech from out back.

"Marylou! You hear me, Marylou? Bring us something to drink!"

"Be right there," I yelled back, wiping my face on my sleeve and opening the refrigerator. I didn't have to wonder what they wanted. The only thing there was to drink was a jug of water and one six-pack, and they sure didn't want the water. Uncle Ed always said water would rust his guts. I figured he was probably right about that. A drink of water would be so unfamiliar to his digestive system, his stomach would surely turn inside out from the shock.

I got two cans of beer and stuffed them into those foam rubber cups that were supposed to keep them cold, then I glanced at the clock. It was only ten-thirty. They were starting earlier than usual, a strong indication that it wasn't going to be a real fine day.

It was hot outside, too, but a tired breath of a breeze stirred the air a little bit, and I thought maybe Sam and I could go for a walk later on, when the sun was low.

They were sitting under the big oak tree in those metal lawn chairs, the kind where the part you lean back on is made to look kind of like a seashell. Half-dead weeds straggled over most of the backyard, but the path out to the shade tree

3

and the area around their chairs was plain beaten-down dirt. Another beaten-down path led from the shade tree out into the weeds a little way. Uncle Ed figured it was a waste of energy to come inside the house every time he had to use the bathroom, not to mention a waste of water flushing the toilet so much. Aunt Bonnie always came inside to use the bathroom. I liked to think she was probably frustrated at that. It was about the only thing she hadn't figured out a way to make me do for her.

"Get yourself on out here, girl," Uncle Ed grumbled. "It's hotter'n a stewed goose, and me'n Bonnie's thirsty." He scratched his big white belly, then settled himself more comfortably in the chair when I handed him his beer.

Uncle Ed bragged every now and then about his thirty-four inch waistline, and I couldn't get over his silliness. I was amazed every time I heard it, but I knew better than to ever say what I was thinking. He hadn't had a waistline in years. Sure, the way he wore his jeans he could wear thirty-fours, but the belly that hung over his "waistline" was more like sixty-four inches. His eyes were squinty and too small for his face, and his hair, what little he had, always looked like a bird's nest, but he actually thought he was attractive.

Of course, to give the devil his due, Uncle Ed thought Aunt Bonnie was attractive, too. "I got me a whole lotta woman here," he would say after he'd had a few. "Yessir, my Bonnie's a mighty sexy broad." And he meant it, too.

Aunt Bonnie was as skinny as a woman could be and stay alive, and except for that, maybe she would have been nice looking if her face hadn't always looked swollen and puffy. She wore too much makeup, too, but I guess she did what she could to keep Uncle Ed thinking she was "a whole lotta woman."

She wasn't in a very good mood that morning. "What you been doin' in there, Marylou?" she demanded. "Ain't you got them dishes done yet? And where's Sam at? You better be keepin' an eye on that boy, not lettin' him get into anything!"

4

"I'm almost finished, and Sam's fine," I said. "He's playing in the bathtub."

"Wastin' water!" Uncle Ed said. "Ain't enough water in the world to make that little brat white."

I despised him when he said dirty things like that. Usually I just disliked him, but lately he'd been saying nasty things about Sam a lot more often. So I disliked him about a third of the time and despised him for the other two-thirds.

But I also knew when to keep quiet unless I was willing to take a chance on getting myself hurt. So I just said, "Gosh, Uncle Ed, it's awful hot, and Sam's just a baby. I only put a couple of inches of water in the tub, and it keeps him happy and cool."

"You get yourself in there and get that brat outta that tub before I slap your smart mouth!" he roared. "And don't be wastin' any more water on him. You know as well as I do them people don't feel the heat like we do!"

I was all the way back inside the house before I realized I was clenching my teeth so hard that my jaws hurt. How I despised that fat slug and his painted skeleton of a wife!

Yet it hadn't always been that way, and while I looked in on Sam and quickly finished the dishes, I couldn't help remembering some of the better times. They were such a contrast!

Uncle Ed had worked at a car manufacturing plant, and although I can still remember that he usually smelled of beer, he'd been kind enough. I remembered Aunt Bonnie hugging me now and then when I was little, and answering my questions about my real parents with gentleness if not much real information.

But Uncle Ed got hurt on the job and collected some kind of financial settlement. They bought the house, and after that neither of them did much of anything. At first they would go out and party or have people at the house, but as time went by, and I suppose as the money dwindled away, they stayed at home more and more, and gradually they fell into the habit

5

of drinking together, day after day. Both of them became increasingly more difficult, and Uncle Ed especially so.

I knew they received a check each month for keeping me. The check came from the government, and I guess it wasn't very much. They got by, paying for utilities and taxes and buying groceries with the help of food stamps. More and more, the housework fell to me, but I was used to spending my time alone anyway, so I didn't mind too much. I escaped the drudgery, in my mind at least, by loving school. There I was silent and I guess withdrawn, but enchanted nevertheless. I was a dreamer. Uncle Ed was right when he called me that.

I had only two more years of high school, and while I was no longer happy in my real world, I knew I would survive. Somehow I would go to college where I would learn and learn, and one day become a famous writer, and all would be well. . . .

And then Sam came.

It was a few days after the end of my sophomore year when Aunt Bonnie told me that we were definitely getting a foster child. By then I knew why without being told, because they'd already told me, in a way.

On a chilly evening a few weeks before, they had been sitting inside drinking beer. It was almost funny the way they sat facing the television set just as if there was something to see besides the dark screen, a blank owlish eye staring back at them. At the table in the kitchen, I struggled over a page of diagramming. I remember that the grammar exercise featured infinitive phrases. In fact, that's what caught my attention to their talk and got me to eavesdropping. It's ridiculous, the way a person's mind works sometimes.

I heard Aunt Bonnie say, "I sure wish we could get the TV fixed, Ed. It ain't much fun to sit here all day with nothin' to do," and I thought, "to sit; that's an infinitive. . . ."

"Ain't much we can do about it," Uncle Ed replied. "You know what the repairman said. Sixty-seven dollars to fix it, and we ain't got much more'n sixty-seven cents."

You've spent at least sixty-seven dollars on beer this month,

I thought. But I didn't say it. I did quit working to listen, though.

"We need more money, Ed," Aunt Bonnie whined, "and I don't know but one honest way to get it."

"How's that?" he asked.

"I done told you the other day," she said.

"Oh, that," he said. "It may be honest, but lord have mercy, Bonnie, do you reckon we could handle another kid? When we took Marylou, it was on account of you bein' lonesome while I was at work. You ain't got that problem no more though."

Aunt Bonnie actually giggled, like some of the silly girls at school, and they were quiet for a few minutes. I figured the conversation was over, but then I heard Uncle Ed say, "Quit your foolin' around, Bonnie, and talk serious. They might stick us with a real problem kid. Then what'd we do?"

"Send him back," she replied. "Gettin' a foster kid ain't the same as adoptin' one. But we could prob'ly get a young one that wasn't old enough to be too troublesome. They's lots of kids need a good home like we got."

"But with a young'un, you'd have to take care of him, and you really ain't got the time, what with the housework and all."

What housework, I wanted to yell. Since when had Aunt Bonnie done any housework? Not for the past couple of years, for sure. It was so stupid I would have laughed, if I hadn't been so aggravated. They were actually serious about pretending that Aunt Bonnie ever did anything around the house, and about getting another foster child. That was just what I needed, somebody else to clean up after!

"I know it," Aunt Bonnie was saying, "but think about it. We'd get twice the money we're gettin' now for Marylou, and prob'ly a third again in food stamps. We could even get the Ford fixed up again, and maybe get outa the house ever' now'n again like we used to do."

"Yeah, I reckon we're gonna hafta do something," Uncle Ed grumbled. "Another kid, though . . . but groceries and utilities are gettin' more expensive ever' day."

7

The price of beer's gone up, too, I thought. But I didn't actually say a word. Uncle Ed was a big man, and he'd been getting more and more quick to slap me around. He never needed much of an excuse.

So that's the way it developed. If it seems unlikely that the state would place another foster child in the care of my foster parents, well, it really wasn't, at least not on the surface. While the house needed paint and some repairs, it really wasn't too bad. I kept the house and the front yard spotless. Uncle Ed could "prove" his disability, making it sort of respectable for him to sit around the house. I was a model student, which was a good recommendation for them, and Uncle Ed and Aunt Bonnie could put on a pretty fair show. Goodness knows they'd had enough practice over the years. When the caseworker from the welfare office was expected, they became ideal foster parents for an hour. Then, too, the caseworker, skinny, eager Mr. Patterson, seemed awfully anxious to see only the positive side of things.

So they got Sam. Or rather, I got Sam, for he was my responsibility from the first moment.

He was a darling, so beautiful! Part white and part Negro, his skin glowed a lovely golden brown, and his eyes—oh, his wonderful sparkling brown eyes! I loved him. Sam held my heart in his chubby little hands before he'd been in the house ten minutes, and he was only two and a half.

The best thing about Sam, though—and I hate to admit this because it's so selfish—was the way he hugged me, snuggled against me, toddled after me, and loved me, loved me, loved me! But he got as good as he gave, because I loved him back with all my heart.

Aunt Bonnie ignored him unless he got in her way or made too much noise. Uncle Ed disliked him from the start. How could anyone dare *not* love my wonderful, beautiful Sam?

Chapter Two

ON THE SEVENTEENTH of August, we'd had Sam for exactly sixty-eight days. I know that's not very long, but—well, you'd just have to see him to understand how he could have become so important to me so quickly. Or maybe you'd have to see me, or get to know me a little bit. I'm no dummy, and I don't have to hear it from a shrink to realize how necessary it is to be loved. Without someone to love me, I feel pretty certain that I would just dry up, just shrink away until there'd be nothing left of what had been me, kind of like the way the leaves shrink and dry up in the fall when winter's coming. That's the way I had been feeling for about two years, before Sam came. All I could feel inside myself was wintertime. But when he wrapped those chubby little arms around my neck and hung on to me for dear life, well, right then I could feel my own self coming back to life, too, and that's the truth.

So you see, it was almost like I had to have Sam or I would die. Before he came, all I had to keep me going was the stories I dreamed up, and I had to keep even that pretty much of a secret. Every time Uncle Ed caught me writing my stories, he would yell at me about how I was wasting my time and ask if there wasn't something useful I could be doing.

But I knew. Somehow I just knew for sure and certain that it wasn't any waste of time, and that someday I would become a real writer. Oh, it would be years and years no doubt, after I'd finished college and gotten a job in New York with a really big publishing company—or maybe, just possibly,

I'd start getting good enough before I'd actually finished college.

It was Miss Worth, my junior high English teacher, who'd told me about the publishing companies, and about how if I really stayed with it, I might get my stories published someday.

"You've got a real flair for storytelling, Marylou," she had told me one cold January day three years before. Her words were music; better than music, they were golden coins, glittering diamonds. . . . I wondered even then if she had any idea what her praise meant to me.

Overwhelmed, not to mention my terrible shyness, all I could say then was "Thank you," but she went on, showing me what was especially good about my writing and what wasn't so good.

"Write about the things you see around you, Marylou," she said. "Better yet, write about the things you feel, the things that make you laugh, and cry. And the things that make you angry, too."

"Those things make good stories?" I asked, doubting. "Those are awfully plain and simple things, not grand and wonderful."

"Oh, but they are grand and wonderful, Marylou," she insisted. "The best, the greatest writing that has ever been done is, right down at the bottom where it counts, about what you're calling the plain and simple things of life."

Still doubting, I stopped writing about the things that came to me in my daydreams, impossibly wonderful and sparkling things, and began making stories like she had suggested. And after a few tries, even I could tell that they were better.

But Miss Worth moved away at the end of my eighth grade year and nobody came to take her place. Oh, I had other English teachers, and they were nice enough, but my heart positively ached sometimes for Miss Worth.

It was Miss Worth I was thinking about when I heard Sam's scream from the bathroom. I nearly jumped out of my skin, then ran for him in terror. He was really crying hard, the kind of crying that tells you for sure that someone is hurt.

I grabbed him from the tub, and I started crying too when I saw the blood. He had evidently stood up in the bathtub, then fallen against the faucet. Blood ran down his face, and I grabbed a towel and wiped it away, terrified to see. Then I could tell that it wasn't so bad as it looked. He had a small cut on his forehead just above his right eye. It wasn't bad; it really wasn't. It was just that there was so much blood!

I wet the corner of the towel and pressed it against the cut to stop the bleeding while I cuddled and comforted Sam, and he had stopped crying and only whimpered a little bit, when Uncle Ed came stomping into the house.

"What's that kid yelling about?" he bellowed, and before I could choke back my own tears enough to answer, he was there in the bathroom doorway.

"I said what's the matter with him!" he yelled again, grabbing my shoulder and spinning me around. I almost dropped Sam, which scared me even worse.

"It's just a little cut," I finally managed. "He's all right. He was mostly just frightened."

"I'll give that brat something to cry about if he don't stop that yellin'!" Uncle Ed growled.

He seemed to have missed the fact that Sam had already stopped crying, but Uncle Ed's anger frightened Sam again, for he clung to me even tighter and began to cry as hard as ever.

Before I could even realize what was happening, Uncle Ed had slapped me on the side of the head, knocking me against the wall, and he jerked Sam from my arms. He held Sam by one arm, and whacked his poor naked bottom about half a dozen times as hard as he could in the cramped space of the bathroom. Then he threw him onto the floor and turned to me. He was actually grinning, while Sam sobbed and screamed in pain and fear.

"That's what you get for not doin' what you're told," he said, "and as for the brat there, now he's got something to cry about!"

11

Aunt Bonnie had followed him inside. I could see her peering around Uncle Ed, and her face looked as if she might be about to cry, too. I always knew, every time Uncle Ed hit me or Sam, that Aunt Bonnie felt bad about it. But as far as I had ever been able to tell, she'd never made one single actual objection. Her sadness never lasted more than a few minutes either. Aunt Bonnie never was what you could call a deep thinker.

Anyway, they went back outside, taking fresh beers with them, and I finally got Sam quieted. Then for a little while I felt like I was two different people at the same time.

I cuddled Sam, talking all the loving nonsense that came to mind while I put a Band-Aid on the cut and dressed him. And all the time, tears ran down my face, and I had to keep wiping my eyes so I could see what I was doing. Every time I looked at his precious face, the tears would gush again, for he gazed at me with those wide, wonderful eyes, and I knew that he must have been trying in his baby way to fathom how his little world could be so peculiar.

But in another part of my mind there was no tenderness and no grief, but only hatred. Sure, Uncle Ed had been knocking me around some—quite a lot lately. But it hadn't been all that bad. Oh, I'd thought about running away or something, but never very seriously. Always, any thought of getting away had been overwhelmed by that bigger dream, of finishing school, then going away to college. . . .

That day something changed. Even while I had despised him, I'd held on to better memories from a few years back, and I'd had some affection if not respect for Uncle Ed.

No more. He had been brutal to Sam, unforgivably brutal, and while I had been able to keep myself from doing so until that day, I could no longer avoid it. I had to try and anticipate our future, Sam's and mine.

Uncle Ed had whipped Sam lots of times, some spankings, some . . . . more than that. But always before it had been sort of casual, kind of an irritated reaction. It had been bad enough, but not exactly *cruel*. I'd known it was wrong to

12

even spank a child his age, but I'd been able to put it out of my mind . . . sort of. Maybe that was because he'd never hit Sam when he was already hurt, or because Sam hadn't been so terrified about the whippings. But this time, Uncle Ed had done it deliberately, even going to the trouble to come inside just for that purpose. And now that he had treated Sam so brutally, and smiled about it, I knew it would continue, because he didn't bother to hide the fact that hitting me gave him pleasure—and he didn't like Sam in the first place. Could I protect him? Not likely. Uncle Ed was getting too unpredictable.

Around and around I went, worrying and wondering. And the only solution I came up with caused me to hurt inside so badly that there's no point in even trying to describe it.

I could get the welfare people to come and get Sam.

Oh God! If I lost him, I would die. And Sam—wouldn't his little heart break, missing me? The thought of his eyes, now so full of fun and love, filling with sorrow he would never be able to understand ripped me apart, and I grew nauseated just thinking of him crying and searching for ''Ma'Lou.'' He might never get over it, for he was just a baby, much too young to know that I hadn't deserted him in my heart, but only for his own physical protection.

It was a drastic step to even consider. Yet when I heard of children who had been left in homes where they were abused, or had been repeatedly returned to the same conditions by the courts, it made me ill.

One thing was clear. I was the only one who loved Sam. And Uncle Ed had just whipped him and thrown him on the floor, a two-and-a-half-year-old, for crying when he was already injured.

Abuse.

I knew that people in ''official'' positions always seemed to have trouble defining the simplest things. I didn't have that difficulty. No matter what a judge might call it, I knew that what Uncle Ed had done was child abuse. And I could be reasonably sure that it would happen again. No matter what,

13

no matter how much it might hurt me, I had a responsibility. Whatever it took, I would try to protect Sam.

I stayed in the house, and I could barely stand to put Sam down even when he squirmed in impatience to get on the floor and play.

Then I heard it again: "Marylou! Bring us a beer!"

There were only two left, not nearly enough to last them till supper time, and when I told them, Uncle Ed said, "Get yourself down to the store and bring back another twelve-pack, and don't be long about it!"

We lived half a mile from town, and it was hot, much too hot to walk and carry a twelve-pack of beer, but I'd done it before. The thing was, I'd always left Sam there with Uncle Ed and Aunt Bonnie. Usually I'd go while he was napping.

But Sam wasn't about to go to sleep then, being so keyed up, and when I thought of leaving him there, I just couldn't do it. What if he started crying? So I decided to take him along, although I couldn't imagine how I'd carry him and the twelve-pack both. Sam could walk of course, but nothing like that kind of distance.

I was already out the door when I made another decision. I would do something I had been trying to work up the courage to do for a long time. I went back inside and got the manila envelope that I had addressed to *Seventeen* magazine weeks before. I took three dollars from my hiding place behind my dresser. Today I would mail my best story. Yet knowing what a waste it was, I could hardly make myself take the money. I'd saved it for so long, until I had accumulated thirty-three dollars. Every time I got a dollar's worth of change, I would take it to town with me and exchange it for a dollar bill. Now I'd be going backward, to thirty dollars.

But I took the money and Sam, and I started walking. Although half a mile isn't really very far, it seemed to take forever. The heat pounded down on us, bouncing back from the paved highway in sickening waves, and before we'd gotten more than halfway there, Sam began to fuss.

"Ma'Lou, Sam t'irsty," he whimpered.

"I know, sweetie," I soothed. "Pretty soon we'll get to town, and we'll get a nice drink."

But Sam didn't understand "pretty soon." "Sam *t'irsty*, Sam *'ot*," he said again, and over and over. He was so miserable. His little body grew wet with perspiration, and he scrubbed his fists into his eyes.

Everything was dry and dead. The scraggly weeds by the roadside exploded puffs of dust when I had to walk there while cars flew past. And Sam grew heavier and harder to carry with every step. How would I ever make it back?

By the time we finally reached the parched and ugly little town, I felt dizzy and my knees trembled. But we got a drink at the first place, a gas station, and since he was damp anyway, I splashed water on Sam's hair and washed his face and arms with my hand cupped full of water. Soon he giggled and jabbered, cool and happy once more, and we went on to the post office.

The envelope containing my story was wrinkled and smudged, and I almost changed my mind. It was a dumb idea in the first place, I told myself. No way in the world would *Seventeen* magazine be interested in publishing a story written by an ignorant fifteen-year-old.

And yet, I was there; the envelope was ready. I had postage money, and if I didn't mail it, I'd have to carry it back home. So I mailed it. It cost a dollar and forty-seven cents.

That done, we went to the combination grocery and liquor store, an overcrowded, rundown place on the other side of town. We had to wait for a while because the owner wouldn't let me buy beer until there was nobody else in the store. It was illegal of course, selling beer to a minor, but he was always nice to me, so I'm not going to use the owner's real name here. I'll call him Mr. Smith.

The waiting bothered me because Uncle Ed would have a fit if I was gone too long. On the other hand, it gave me a chance to rest for a while in the shade, and Sam a little time to play before we started back.

Finally the store was empty, and Mr. Smith quickly put the beer in a brown bag.

"It's on sale today, Marylou," he said pleasantly. "You're gonna save your Uncle Ed a couple of dollars."

"That's nice," I said. I wanted to leave right then, but he kept talking. I didn't want to be rude; he was always so friendly.

"How's the little one getting along?" he asked, patting Sam's cheek.

"Oh, he's fine, Mr. Smith," I said. "I'm crazy about him."

"You know, he even looks a little like you," Mr. Smith mused, gazing at us curiously. "I mean, I know he's a foster child and that he's part Negro and all that, but what I mean is, you do have that curly black hair, not like his of course, but . . . and you're so tan . . . I didn't mean anything Marylou," he kind of mumbled, embarrassed, thinking he'd offended me.

"Gosh, that's okay," I hurried to assure him. "I don't mind. In fact, I think it's kind of neat, you thinking we look alike."

"Not really, not all that much, I mean . . . just sort of," he said. Then he changed the subject to something more comfortable.

"Anxious for school to start?" he asked.

"I sure am," I said. "It's been a long summer."

We talked a little more about school, then I said that I'd better be getting back.

"You're not walking, surely," he asked, looking worried.

"Oh no," I lied. I only lied when it was a question of pride. "I've got a ride," I said. "Uncle Ed wouldn't let me walk so far, especially bringing Sam along."

"Well, all right then, if you're sure," Mr. Smith said, and for the first time, I had the feeling that he didn't believe me.

From the money saved on beer, I paid myself back the dollar and forty-seven cents. Then we started back.

That walk back—it was so bad that I hate even remembering it. With Sam in one arm and the twelve-pack under the other, it was murder. Then to make things worse, Sam got irritable and grumpy. He was getting sleepy, which made

16

him harder to carry, and it wasn't long before he started whimpering again.

"Sam *t'irsty*. Sam *'ot*," he whimpered. Over and over and over.

I kept going until I felt my arms would give way any second, but finally I *had* to stop and rest. A half-dead tree provided a sketchy bit of shade, and I dropped to the ground, gasping with pain when I placed Sam and the beer on the ground at last. I rubbed my aching arms, which didn't help very much, then fell onto my back in the weeds.

"Sam *t'irsty*. Sam *'ot*," he whimpered again, climbing onto my stomach and patting my face.

I couldn't stand it. I called Uncle Ed every name I could think of, but that didn't help either. Sam was hot and tired and thirsty and so was I. But there wasn't anything to drink.

Then my outstretched hand brushed against the twelve-pack, and it felt so good, still cold even. The paper bag was damp from the sweating cans inside.

I could give Sam a drink of the beer. The taste was foul of course. I'd tasted it before and knew it to be repulsive. But it was cold, and it was wet.

I opened a can, intending to let him drink some. He was so thirsty, and surely a little drink of the beer wouldn't hurt. Then I thought of what beer had done to my own life, and Sam's, and I could not give it to him. In only another fifteen minutes, I could give him a drink of water at home.

I wanted to take a sip, myself. How wonderfully wet and cold it felt! I turned the can up to drink, but the spoiled smell was more than I could bear. I turned it upside down and watched the parched earth drink up the foaming liquid. That was my childhood, I thought. Beer. All it left behind was ugly feelings . . . and a bad smell.

I don't recall much about the rest of that walk because it was so miserable, but we made it home, and I was quick to get the beer out of the box and into the refrigerator so the missing can wouldn't be noticed. I fixed supper somehow,

17

while my foster parents had another beer apiece before they came inside to eat. Soon afterward, they went to bed.

My head throbbed a little from the heat and exhaustion, but at last I got Sam into bed, too.

Then the worries came back. It had been pretty good there for a little while. Still exhausted from the terrible walk, I'd had all I could manage, just getting the meal fixed and everything, and my fears had vanished for a time.

But now they were back, and a new element came to torture me. It had been nagging at the edge of my thoughts since Mr. Smith had mentioned school. I hadn't really thought about it, but school would be starting in just three more weeks. What would happen to Sam while I was in school?

It was too much. I relived that horrible few moments of the afternoon, and I knew it would happen again. When I went off to school, Sam would be sure to cry for me. And when he started to cry, irritating Uncle Ed . . . I knew what would happen.

I won't go into all the agonizing I did that evening. I'll just make the story short. We had a telephone, though it was rarely used. It was required by the welfare people I suppose. I went to the phone, sick at heart, and I called the social worker, Mr. Patterson, at his home.

"Why Marylou," he exclaimed when I identified myself, "how nice to hear from you. You're all right, aren't you?"

"I'm all right Mr. Patterson," I said quietly, "but there's a problem here that I need to tell you about."

"A problem; oh dear," he said, sounding flustered. Then, "How can I help you, Marylou?"

"It's Sam really," I said.

"Sam? He's not sick I hope."

"No," I said, "he isn't sick . . . that is . . ." I stopped, unsure how I should continue. I began to wish that I had prepared myself a little better.

"Well then," Mr. Patterson said, "what is it?" I could sense a note of suspicion in his voice. Then when I didn't reply right away, he went on. "Surely you're not objecting to having Sam there. It takes awhile, Marylou, to accustom yourself to having a small child around. Be patient; you'll get used to it. Probably you'll even come to love him if you'll give it a little more time."

After that I didn't have so much trouble knowing what to say, for I was angry. But I had to talk quietly. It wasn't at all likely, but it was possible that Uncle Ed or Aunt Bonnie would wake up.

"I already love Sam, Mr. Patterson," I said. "He's the best thing that's ever happened to me. It's Uncle Ed and Aunt Bonnie. If *they* loved him, we'd be all right. But they don't, especially Uncle Ed. He hates Sam, Mr. Patterson. He's cruel to Sam."

"Cruel?" he asked, clearly astonished and unbelieving. "Oh, come now, my dear. Surely you're overreacting. I can't imagine Ed Stark abusing any child. Why, look what a fine foster parent he's been to you! Why don't you just tell me what's happened, and we'll go from there and clear up this . . . this misunderstanding."

I can't say that I *knew* what was going to happen then, but I did have a pretty clear idea. He had already made up his mind. But I told him about the beating anyway. When I had finished, Mr. Patterson was quiet for a couple of minutes. I waited, scared of what he would say.

"First of all," he finally said, "it sounds to me as if you've gotten much too attached to Sam."

I could have screamed. He sounded like we were talking about a puppy. Just a minute before, he'd been implying that I resented Sam, and now I was "too attached" to him. How could anyone love a child too much? But Mr. Patterson wasn't finished.

"It seems obvious that you are overdramatizing what happened," he said. "If the department hadn't trusted Ed's and Bonnie's judgment, neither you nor Sam would have been placed in their home, and . . ."

"But Mr. Patterson, you don't understand," I interrupted, unable to keep the desperation out of my voice. "Sam's only a baby. Nobody should *ever* hit a baby!"

19

"You said Ed hit him several times," Mr. Patterson said. "How many times, exactly?"

"Well, I didn't *count*," I said, "but it was at least six or . . ."

"Did he use his fists?"

"No," I said. "No, he didn't. He was holding him by one arm, Mr. Patterson, and he . . ."

"So what really happened is that your Uncle Ed spanked Sam on his bottom, with his open hand. Isn't that it?"

"Well . . . in a way," I stammered, so upset I could hardly think, "but Mr. Patterson, you really don't understand. The point is that Sam's just a baby, and Uncle Ed doesn't like him, and . . ."

"Marylou, perhaps you're right in thinking a child Sam's age shouldn't receive corporal punishment," Mr. Patterson butted in. "But parents *do* make mistakes, you know; be a little forgiving. And caring for a small child can really try a father's patience. However, that's hardly the issue. An open-handed spanking doesn't begin to constitute child abuse, dear."

Dear! If he'd been there in person, I swear he would've been patting me on the head. How any supposedly grown man could be so dense was beyond me. He hadn't really listened to a thing I had said; he'd heard only what he had preferred to hear, and I knew I could not penetrate that kind of wall. So when he suggested that he just might be able to find a moment to spare from his busy schedule so that he could come out the next day and "Help us all smooth out our little misunderstandings," I told him not to bother. He didn't argue; it was clear that he was relieved.

"But you be sure and call me just anytime you feel the need to talk to someone, Marylou," he gushed. "That's what I'm here for, you know, to help my people in any way I can. Don't ever forget that I'm your friend."

I'll get him a dictionary for Christmas, I thought, so he can learn what the words "help" and "friend" mean. And in the meantime, I could darn sure do without his help and friendship!

The touble was, after talking with Mr. Patterson, I knew for certain that I was on my own. It was going to be just Sam and me.

Chapter Three

I WISH I could skip this part.

I can't do it though, because without the truth about the few hours after I talked to Mr. Patterson, the rest of the story wouldn't make any sense. Come to think of it, it might not make a whole lot of sense anyway.

I was so terribly depressed. Every magazine or newspaper seemed to contain horror stories about abused children, or articles about the prevention of child abuse. Yet here we were, Sam and me, and I could see it coming, see it in Sam's future as clear as daylight, and the man who had put Sam in the situation wouldn't even listen—would never listen unless something really unthinkable happened. Then it would be too late.

Perhaps that explained why so many children suffered such awful things every day, I thought—somebody like Mr. Patterson refusing to listen to something he didn't want to know.

But refusing to hear wouldn't make the bad things go away. I knew that, but I didn't know what to do about it!

I'm not saying that what happened next was Mr. Patterson's fault, because it wasn't. I do believe he was partly responsible, but I can't blame it on him; I have to face the truth. Mr. Patterson didn't do it. I did.

I thought on and on, remembering every ugly detail of the day. All the memories came back, mixing with scenes of my childhood that I'd thought forgotten, scenes of loneliness and rejection and emptiness. These memories began somehow to grow and to magnify. Pretty soon Uncle Ed and Aunt Bonnie were no longer just insensitive and selfish and a little bit cruel; they became monsters, in my mind, capable of horrendous, atrocious crimes. . . .

I recalled Sam's screams, and the tears flowed in rivers down my face. I, who so rarely cried, trembled and sobbed and became as shaky as an ancient crone.

I had long understood that life was often unfair, that the good things weren't exactly distributed evenly. I knew the world was full of unpleasant things, of hungry people and bitterness and pain. But having that kind of objective knowledge is not like experiencing those things, not at all. For anyone to actually despise a child . . . for anyone to willingly ignore a child's danger rather than admit his own error . . . to see and experience what must surely be the most unforgivable of sins, was intolerable to me.

After that, my recollection is pretty sketchy, but the thing that matters is that I somehow came to the conclusion that the only thing to do was to take Sam and run away with him.

So that is what I did.

I put a few things into my school backpack: one change of clothes, a comb, a bar of soap and a washcloth, three changes of clothes plus extra training pants for Sam, a few cookies and crackers, and an orange-juice jug full of water. I put my thirty-three dollars and a few more things in my jeans pockets, then pulled another pair of jeans and shirt over my clothes. I got Sam out of bed without waking him, and started walking down the highway in the opposite direction from town.

Common sense will tell you that the first person who saw us or stopped to give us a ride would call someone, or take us straight to the police station or some similar thing. But common sense wasn't in control on the seventeenth of August.

Sam was heavy. I couldn't believe how much heavier he seemed while he was sleeping, but the backpack balanced his weight a little bit, so it wasn't too bad. I was in a state of hysteria and I don't know how far I walked; surely not very far. The only thing I remember real clearly is when I saw this car pulled over on the side of the road. It scared me, because at that point my brain had started a sputtery kind of functioning again, and I imagined all sorts of possibilities: A psychotic murderer was sitting there in that car; it was an unmarked highway patrol car; it was someone who would recognize me and call Uncle Ed. . . .

The car was empty though. Later I realized that it must've broken down, and the driver had gone somewhere for assistance.

My head began to feel puffed up and hollow, not really hurting, but miserable just the same. My mouth was dry as dust, and I wanted a drink of water. But I'd have to put Sam down and take off the backpack to get a drink, so I kept going.

And in a little while, this big eighteen-wheeler stopped, and the passenger door swung open.

"Your car break down, lady?" a scratchy voice asked from 'way above me. "Get in; that young'n must be gettin' mighty heavy by now."

I was puzzled; what was this man talking about? Then I remembered the car by the roadside, and I decided to go along with his assumption. I knew I couldn't walk much farther, and the big truck looked so wonderfully *secure*.

With the driver's help, I managed to get myself, Sam, and the backpack into the cab of the truck. The driver was heavy-set and gray haired, and his voice, though very deep, sounded pleasantly friendly to me.

I'd made absolutely no plans. I'd been out of my mind when I decided to run away, and I hadn't had a really rational thought since. Where was I going? I had no idea. How had I figured on getting there? The trouble was, I hadn't "figured" at all! It was some fine mess I'd gotten myself and Sam into.

Surely the truck driver would see that I was just a kid, then he'd know something was wrong.

He didn't, though. There wasn't much light inside the cab of the truck, but he peered at me and gently touched Sam's cheek with one finger. "He's a fine boy," he said. "Looks a lot like his mama too, don't he?"

Mama? This man thought Sam was my son! Then my fuzzy brain recognized what a break that was. Maybe I did look older than fifteen and a half, and it was pretty dark, and after all, even thirteen-year-olds have babies.

So I said, "Thanks. Sam's a wonderful baby all right. Lots of people say he looks like me."

"Where were you headed?" he asked then. "Swifton? That's where I'm unloading."

What could I say? I knew Swifton was about a hundred miles away, and it was a good-sized town. Why not?

"Yes," I told him. "My sister lives in Swifton. Sam and I are going to visit her for a week. I'm really glad for the ride."

Then he said, "What'll you do about your car?"

Oh boy. By then my head had begun to pound, and I couldn't think. My brain seemed full of bumblebees. Yet somehow I found an answer.

"I was sort of hoping you'd be willing to stop at a service station, so I can call my uncle," I said. "He'll come and get the car for me."

"Sure, I reckon that'll be okay," he said.

At the next station he pulled in, I faked a phone call, then got back inside the truck. I was so tired I barely knew what I was doing, and my head felt as if it might fall off every time we hit a bump, which was about every three seconds. Sam came halfway awake a couple of times, until I finally laid him in the seat; then he settled down and slept peacefully. He didn't seem to feel the bumps that were tearing the top half of my head off.

I'd never felt so out of touch with reality. I was scared; what in the world could be wrong with me, I wondered. Was I going to die?

Of course I didn't die. Instead, I went to sleep.

* * *

The next thing I knew, the truck driver was shaking me by the shoulder. I came awake slowly, barely aware of who or where I was, with my head aching and hollow. My neck and shoulders felt so tight that a touch could have shattered the bones.

"Time to wake up, young lady," the driver said. "We'll be in Swifton in a few minutes. Do you have cab fare to get to your sister's? I can't drive this rig on the residential streets."

Mumbling, my mouth full of rubber, I tried to answer him. Then I saw the city limit sign: Swifton, population 124,000. And a few yards past the sign, a graveled road turned off to the right.

"Stop here," I said quickly. "My sister lives just a little way down this road. It won't be a bit of trouble for me to walk that far."

He stopped, though he had to back up a few feet. Then he helped me out of the cab. I got the backpack in place, and he put Sam in my arms, still sleeping. The moon glowed brightly, and the lights from the truck illuminated all of us, and I could see that the truck driver looked troubled.

"Are you sure you'll be all right?" he asked, his heavy brows drawing together in a frown. "It's almost two o'clock in the morning, you know."

"We'll be fine," I said, even though by that time what I wanted was to tell him the whole truth and ask him what I should do. But it wasn't his problem, and he had already gone to so much trouble for us. I opened my mouth to say something, but all that came out was, "We'll be fine, and my sister will be waiting up for us. I certainly appreciate your help."

"Well, all right, if you're sure," the man said, "but young lady . . . would you mind listening to a bit of advice from an old man?"

"Of course I don't mind," I said. And he wasn't an old man, either.

"The next time your car breaks down," he said, "just stay there till daylight or until a patrolman stops. It's not safe for you to be walking, especially when you've got a responsibility like this little guy. Will you remember that?''

"I'll remember," I said, and I meant it with all my heart. In spite of the sleepiness and the headache and the fear that was starting to nudge me in the pit of my stomach, I was at last beginning to get a glimpse of what a foolish and dangerous thing I had done.

At least I thought I was beginning to see. What I didn't know yet was that my learning had barely even begun!

Chapter Four

I CAME AWAKE reluctantly. Although I wasn't really *thinking* about it, it was as though my unconscious mind knew that there were problems too big for me to face; if I could go on sleeping, the thinking could be postponed.

But when a two-and-a-half-year-old wakes up, whoever's taking care of him wakes up, too, like it or not. Sam climbed all over me, patting my face and talking. My brain was so foggy, it took awhile before I comprehended who or where I was, or what Sam was saying.

"Sam *'ungry*," he said. "Ma'Lou, Sam 'ungry. Sam go *pee*."

That got through the fog, and I sat up. When I did, my head swam. For a moment I could only sit there holding my head in place. Then the dizziness began to recede, and I opened my eyes.

In other circumstances, our surroundings would have been fun and interesting. The cavernous barn I had staggered into during the night had a peculiar musty smell, but it wasn't unpleasant. It was warm and dry, and the rays of light streaming through the cracks between boards gave the place a cheerful, welcoming look. The barn appeared to be about half filled with bales of hay, and the rest of the area was littered with loose, sweet-smelling hay, too. I supposed that the owner came regularly to take hay out to feed his cows, and I wondered for a brief moment what I would say to explain our presence if he showed up right then.

But I couldn't worry about that just then. Sam had to go to the bathroom—if it wasn't already too late.

I knew I should take him outside, but I couldn't face that yet, so I took him to the farthest corner and let that suffice for a bathroom; for myself, too.

He was also hungry. So was I, starving in fact, but my stomach felt awfully shaky. I dug the cookies, the crackers, and the jug of water out of my backpack, and Sam clapped his hands, laughing at the sight of the food.

Poor baby! He didn't know that a dozen or so broken cookies and only a few more crackers wasn't exactly a nutritious meal. Or that when that was gone, I had no idea where I would get more food.

He gobbled cookies and crackers, and he loved drinking out of the orange-juice jug. He kept asking for more, until I knew that it was the novelty of the container he wanted, rather than the water itself.

Then he wanted to play, of course. It didn't matter to Sam that we were a hundred miles from home with thirty-three dollars and a handful of food, trespassing in someone's barn. He loved it! He explored every inch and tried to climb up onto the hay.

I played with him, putting everything else out of my mind. The few crackers I had eaten had calmed my stomach, and the headache was finally only a moderate throbbing.

I didn't have a watch, and had no idea how much time had passed until Sam began to get sleepy. Evidently the strangeness of our surroundings wasn't going to interfere with his schedule. He nearly always took a nap just awhile before noon.

I spread my clean change of clothes on a nice clump of hay, and Sam sprawled on the makeshift bed happily. He gazed up in wonder, reaching for the streams of sunlight. His eyes closed at last as he murmured, "Pretty, pretty lights, Ma'Lou. Pretty, pretty lights."

How indescribably wonderful that a little kid could so easily be happy! I felt grateful that Sam had no fear, no feelings of emptiness, no aching wondering about what to do next. I

29

wasn't so fortunate. Worse, I had done this awful thing my-self, and I had to figure out what to do.

I moved over to the wall and looked through the cracks. The barn stood in a kind of corral, but the fence was falling down in several places. To my left I could see a house. It too was old and appeared deserted, though the windows were covered. Whatever covered them didn't look much like cur-tains from my viewpoint, but more like newspapers that had been pasted to the glass on the inside. It was a small place with a high-pitched roof. Some kind of material made to look like bricks but obviously not the real thing covered the out-side walls, and a little sagging porch in front seemed to be littered with dead leaves and grass. To one side of the house I could see an old-fashioned, rusty water pump. I wondered if it worked. Probably not.

What was I going to do?

It ran through my mind like a stuck record, over and over and over. But it was just a question. I didn't get any answers.

So I went to sleep. I can't explain it. Even now I wonder how I did that. How could I just lie down and go to sleep when I was in such a desperate situation? Even at home where I was safe, I'd lie sleepless when some problem nagged at me, yet in that unfamiliar and potentially dangerous place, I went to sleep!

Sam and I awoke at the same time, and we went through the same ritual: bathroom, then food, then play until he had worn off some of his energy. By then it was past the middle of the afternoon, and we were no better off. Worse, in fact, because the food and water were almost gone.

I couldn't put it off any longer, so while I more or less entertained Sam, I made a mental list of the possibilities.

We could walk back to the highway and hitch a ride home. But I remembered the truck driver's warning, and my own fear when I'd first seen that car by the roadside, and I knew I wouldn't do that. It was too dangerous, and even if I'd been willing to take a risk for myself, I couldn't endanger Sam any more than I had already done. I no longer had the excuse

30

of being so emotionally shaken up, thank God, and I vowed that I would never again, as long as I lived, let my fears overwhelm my common sense.

I could walk into town, or to the nearest house, and say that I had taken Sam out for a walk and we'd been kidnapped. For quite some time I tried to convince myself that would be the best. We would be taken back home, and I wouldn't get into *too* much trouble. But what if that truck driver heard of it and told what had really happened? Then when it occurred to me that the man who had given us a ride and been so nice might even be accused . . . that stopped my thinking about that possibility.

Maybe I could go into Swifton and somehow convince somebody that I was all alone except for Sam, my son . . . maybe I could get a job. But although I daydreamed a bit about that, about having a place just for Sam and me, and earning a living for us, I knew it was a dream and nothing more. It could never happen. I was a kid; nobody would hire me. And besides, what would I do with Sam while I worked, even if I did somehow manage to get a job?

All the time while I considered these things, I was uncomfortably aware of a picture in the back of my mind. It was the memory of something I had seen back in the winter, on a school field trip: a picture of a solid steel door with a narrow slit cut into it, just big enough to stick four fingers through.

We had been taken to visit a correctional school for teenage girls, and I could never forget what I had seen there. That was the idea, I suppose—that we would remember the experience and keep ourselves out of trouble, for fear of being sent there.

We had visited one "cottage" where about twenty girls lived. There were locks on every door. The matrons carried heavy key rings; you could always hear those keys jingling.

The part that horrified me was the individual girl's rooms. We were taken into the room of a girl who had just returned from working in the laundry. She stood against one wall, with her hands cupped together in front of her. She was very nervous and looked as if she was frightened.

The room was tiny. A cot with a thin mattress was bolted to the floor against one wall. A metal desk/dresser stood against the other wall. On a hanger that couldn't be taken off the wall, a single dress hung. It was green cotton, more of a uniform than a dress. The girl wore an identical dress in a faded pink color.

A shiny steel bowl with a rounded edge sat beneath the bed; the girls were allowed two trips to the bathroom each day, we were told. The rest of the time, that shiny bowl served as a toilet. A steel plate was bolted onto the wall. It served as a mirror, the girl who "lived" there said when our escort told her to explain.

The psychologist who escorted us through the place told us that in the evenings after supper, the girls were allowed one hour of television in a "living room" that was bare of everything except couches and a television set. Then they went to the bathroom for showers—five minutes each, no more—then to their rooms. They had to place all their clothes, including shoes, outside their doors on little stools. This, the man said, was because girls had been known to try to kill themselves by hanging, using bra straps, shoestrings, and such. When one of the kids from my school asked whether any girls had succeeded in committing suicide, the psychologist didn't answer.

After their clothes were checked by the matron, the doors were locked, and the girls remained in their rooms till morning.

If one of them got sick or something, they had one way, and only one way to ask for help. They would stick their four fingers through the slit of the door and hope the matron on duty would see. They were not permitted to call out.

It was terrible, an impossible way for a teenaged girl to live. I shivered in horror and couldn't wait to get away. But the worst was still to come.

I was at the end of the line, and the girl who occupied that room tapped my shoulder. I turned to face her. She was tiny, and so awfully thin. Her eyes seemed too big for her thin face, and I've never seen anyone so sad.

"Do you know what butterflies eat?" she whispered to me.

I shook my head, amazed. Had I misunderstood her? What a peculiar question for such a time and place!

Then she opened her hands, which had been cupped together all that time, and nodded for me to see what she had. I looked into her hands. There sat a tiny yellow butterfly.

"I caught it on the way back from the laundry," the girl whispered. "It's just so lonely here . . . and I don't know how to feed it."

My throat ached, and my eyes burned with tears. I could only shake my head again. "I'm sorry," I finally managed to whisper. "I wish I could help you."

Then I had to follow the others out, and the click of the lock on that poor girl's door rang in my ears like the sound of a heart breaking in two.

If I did the right thing, went somewhere and confessed the truth of what I had done, I would be sent to just such a place; the exact *same* place, almost certainly!

It hurt to do it, but I deliberately recalled everything I had seen at that reform school. It was terrible, and I didn't think my fears were exaggerated; most likely I would be sent there. After all, Sam was not my son. He wasn't even really my little brother. So what I had done was kidnapping, and it was certain that Mr. Patterson wouldn't be helpful. In fact, he would probably be glad to sacrifice me, to save his own reputation. Self-centered weakling that he was . . . he'd be no help to me.

Could I stand to live in such a place? Other girls endured it, and I decided I could take it, too. I had meant no harm, had only wanted to save my beautiful Sam from being whipped for no reason except Uncle Ed's whim. But Mr. Patterson hadn't seen it my way; neither would anyone else.

All right, maybe I deserved reform school. A sensible girl doesn't run away in the middle of the night with an innocent child. Maybe I should do what I knew was right, at least in most ways. Maybe I should confess and take my punishment.

Then what would happen to Sam? Would they find a good home for him, where he would be loved and cared for, where someone would hold him and kiss his hurts, and play with him?

If I could be sure of that . . . but the hurt of losing him was nearly more than I could bear to think about. Maybe if I did give myself up, Sam would never again be loved and hugged. . . .

In fact, they'd probably leave him right where he had been, with Uncle Ed and Aunt Bonnie!

Chapter Five

SAM AND I spent another night in the barn, and we were lucky. Nobody bothered us at all. A couple of times that evening I thought I heard noises, and once I could have sworn that a light, like a flashlight beam, raked across the outside of the barn. But every time I went to look through the cracks, I saw nothing. It had only been my imagination, spurred by my fear and insecurity.

It was pleasant in the barn. We had quiet there. There was nobody yelling for me to do this or bring that, and no fear for Sam's immediate safety. Even knowing that autumn would come soon, followed by a cold winter season, I daydreamed of being able to stay there. Oh, I knew better of course, but dreams . . . I can't escape them. Daydreaming is as natural to me as breathing, and usually they're far from sensible.

I cleaned both of us up as well as I could. It was Monday morning, and we were going to walk into town. I knew it probably wouldn't be far to some place where I could get us something to eat. After that, I supposed that I would call someone—the sheriff, maybe, or Family Services—and tell the truth.

We walked back out to the highway, and I took my time, letting Sam toddle along at his own pace. It went pretty slowly because he found countless things to gaze at or to put into his pockets. Sam wasn't afraid of anything. He wanted to catch the grasshoppers that flitted among the grass and weeds, but they were too quick for him. I told him what they were.

"Grasshoppers, Sam," I said. "Can you say that? Grass-hoppers."

"G'ashopper," he mimicked easily. He was so smart, and I loved the way he would think for a couple of seconds, as though almost tasting the new word. Then his little mouth would kind of shape itself around the word, and he'd try it. The result was often funny but nearly always quite accurate.

"Sam get g'ashopper," he said, running after another one and clapping his hands with glee when it escaped.

My thoughts wandered for a moment, then I realized he was tugging at my leg.

"Sam get g'ashopper," he said impatiently. "Ma'Lou see! Sam get g'ashopper!"

I looked down, and he held a dry locust hull up to me. The locust had shed its skin, leaving the hollow shell with the head and leg parts empty but intact. He wanted me to take it, but I could never stand to touch such things. I started to tell him it was a locust, then thought better of it. To Sam it looked like a grasshopper, and he was proud of having "caught" it.

"Sam eat?" he asked, moving the locust hull toward his mouth.

"No, you mustn't eat it," I said quickly, shuddering at the very thought.

"Pocket?" he asked then.

"All right," I said. "Put it in your pocket if you want to." He did so, and went happily chasing after another grass-hopper.

By the time we reached the highway, Sam had tired, and I picked him up and carried him. Soon we were in the out-skirts of Swifton, and I kept walking, looking for a fast-food place or a little store. We passed several eating places, sea-food restaurants and steak houses, but they weren't exactly in our price range.

Then we found just the place we needed, a little store that even had a picnic table under a tree outside. The table was occupied by a boy about my age, but perhaps he'd be gone soon. We went inside, where I bought two little cartons of milk, some bread and cheese, and a shiny red apple for Sam.

I wanted to wait until the boy had gone, but Sam had seen the food, and he was impatient. So we went over to the picnic table anyway.

"May we sit here?" I asked the boy.

"Sure. Help yourself," he replied.

While I opened a carton of milk for Sam and fixed us a sandwich, I watched the boy. He was drinking milk, too, and he had a couple of little bakery cakes. He wasn't bad looking, except that he needed a haircut—and a shampoo, too, for that matter. He wore faded jeans and shabby tennis shoes, and a denim jacket with all kinds of things written on it in ink. There were names of several rock groups, and things like, "This side up," and "Keep your hands off my jacket," and such.

I knew he was watching me too of course, and finally he spoke.

"Cute kid," he said. "Is he yours?"

"Yeah," I said.

"Doesn't look much like you," he observed carefully. Then, "I'm Danny. Give the kid some of this cake if you want."

"Thanks," I said. "Maybe after he eats his sandwich."

"Must be your kid," Danny said then. "You talk like a mama anyway. What's your name?"

"I'm Marylou," I said. "His name is Sam."

"Where you headed, Marylou?"

"Why . . . nowhere really," I replied. "Why?"

"Curious, that's all," he said. "It's obvious you're traveling. What're you running away from?"

"I'm not running away from anything," I replied, troubled at his quick assumption. "What makes you think so?"

He shrugged. "Takes one to know one, as they say. You got real food. Nutritious stuff: cheese, milk, apple. You'da probably bought junk food if you were just loafing. Then there's the backpack, and you're wearing two shirts, and it's too hot for that."

"Lots of people carry backpacks," I said.

"Yeah, sure. But not stuffed full. But don't worry," he went on, "the cops'll never notice. In this town they're blind. Or more likely, they're just not interested."

I didn't know what to say, so I busied myself with Sam, encouraging him to finish his milk. We were quiet for a while. The streets were busy though, with cars swarming, horns, all the city noises.

The boy had finished, leaving half a cake wrapped in paper. But he stayed. For some reason I was glad. It felt kind of nice to be near someone my own age.

He watched us frankly, and finally he spoke again. "Listen," he said, "I ain't bugging you, but . . . have you got a place to crash, or not?"

"Not really," I replied, knowing I might as well admit what he already knew. "I guess I'll just call somebody—go back home."

"If you're gonna go back, why'd you bother to leave in the first place?" he asked.

I thought about it for a minute, and then I told him the truth. He seemed okay, and I did want to tell someone what I'd done. I finished by telling him my fears about reform school.

He thought it over. "It's hard to tell," he said at last. "You can't count on much of anything. Some places, they'd just send you back where you came from and try to forget about you and the kid. Other places, you're right. They'd pack you off to jail. For your own good, of course," he finished with a sneer.

"You're not exactly encouraging," I told him. "What would you do, in my place?"

"It ain't easy to say," he replied. "I'd feel the same as you do, where the kid's concerned."

"His name is Sam," I interrupted.

"Okay," he said with a grin so quick I wasn't sure I'd seen it. "Okay, where Sam is concerned. They wouldn't treat him right. According to what you've said, they'd probably leave him with your . . . what'd you call them?"

38

"Uncle Ed and Aunt Bonnie," I said. "They aren't really my kinfolks though. I'm a foster child, just like Sam."

"Where's your folks?" he asked.

"I don't know anything about them," I said. "Aunt Bonnie said they just left me with the welfare people and disappeared. I was pretty little. I don't remember anything about it."

"You wanta find them?"

"Heck no," I said. "I used to think I did, but I got over it. Why would I care? They deserted me, which sort of suggests they weren't real crazy about having a daughter."

He nodded. "Well then, what're you gonna do?" he asked. He didn't seem terribly concerned, but just curious and interested, which made the talking easy.

"I don't know," I said. "I guess I'd risk reform school for myself, if I could be sure about Sam."

"Yeah, that's the tough part," he agreed. He sat thinking for a while longer. Then he looked me square in the eye. "You got any money?" he asked.

"Thirty dollars," I said, surprised that I'd told him.

"That ain't much, but it'll help," he said. "Tell you what," he went on. "Go back in the store and buy ten dollars worth of stuff. Get stuff like Vienna sausage mostly. Maybe a box of crackers. And a few candy bars. I'll go with you. Then you put the rest of your money in your inside pockets." He was already getting to his feet.

"But what . . . ?" I started to ask.

"A bunch of us have a place," he said. "It ain't much, but you can stay awhile. But it'll help if you bring food with you. Just keep quiet about the twenty bucks you'll have left. If anybody asks, tell 'em you're broke."

I did as Danny said. I did need time to think, after all, and shelter for myself and Sam. I couldn't imagine just what Danny had meant, but I supposed that he and some friends had a house where they shared expenses. The whole idea made me pretty nervous, but he assured me that Sam and I would be welcome. "And there's a couple of girls there, too," he said, "so you won't be the only one."

39

We went into the store, and Danny showed me what to buy. He added up the prices as we selected things, and we stopped when I'd spent just under ten dollars.

While we were there, I saw something that bothered me pretty badly. Danny slipped a pack of cigarettes and a couple of candy bars into his jacket pockets while we shopped. He was awfully smooth about it.

When we went to the checkout counter, he asked the cashier to exchange what remained of my money for five-dollar bills. Once outside, he explained.

"Put each of these bills in different places," he said. "One inside each sock maybe, one in each front jeans pocket. That way if you get ripped off, you won't lose it all."

Then he started emptying his pockets into the grocery bag. I couldn't believe it; he had four packs of cigarettes ("I don't smoke, but Susie does," he explained), half a dozen candy bars, and about a dozen sticks of beef jerky.

"The beef jerky's expensive when you buy it," he said, "but it's good to have when you're moving around. Lasts a long time, gives you something to chew on so you don't get so hungry."

Wow! Danny must've been on his own for a long time, I thought. He sure did seem to know how to survive.

He carried the groceries and my backpack, and I carried Sam. "It's quite a way to our place," he said, "about twenty blocks or so."

When we'd gone about halfway, we came to another little hole-in-the-wall grocery store. He put the stuff he was carrying down, and asked me for some change. I gave it to him, about seventy-five cents. He went into the store and came back out with two packs of gum, one of which he gave to me. He kept the other one. Then again he started digging things out of his pockets: more gum, more beef jerky, and a lollipop for Sam.

I didn't know what to think. He was stealing and I didn't like it. It was wrong, and it scared me. I didn't say anything, but he did. "I'd rather not steal," he said, "although I'm good at it. But I haven't had any work lately, and I have to help support the family. Everybody helps, any way they can."

"Family?" I asked.

"It's just an easy way of saying it," he said. "I've been there nearly a month. People come and go, and everybody's welcome if they bring food in and aren't too weird."

It sounded like what I had read about communes, and I didn't feel too good about it. Would the "family" he spoke so casually about be nice people, or kids on drugs and stuff, or what? I needed some place to go, and I knew that I was going to at least have a look . . . but what in the world was I getting myself into now?

Chapter Six

DANNY'S "FAMILY" LIVED in a house on the west side of town, in what had to be the seediest part of Swifton. The house had NO TRESPASSING signs plastered all over it, but Danny said they knew the owner lived on the west coast and wasn't interested in the place.

It was no wonder. The place was a wreck. It hadn't been occupied, except by those who currently stayed there, in years. Several windows had been replaced with cardboard. There was no electricity. The front and back porches were falling apart. The yard hadn't been mowed, but they had made an effort to clean it up some. They'd chopped the weeds down somehow, and collected all the trash in a big pile out back, next to the old outhouse. With so many people and one inside bathroom, they also used the old-fashioned outside toilet. It too was pretty shabby, but still standing at least. It leaned at such an angle that the door wouldn't close all the way, so when anyone had to use that "bathroom," he had to call out before he got there, to see whether it was already occupied.

Inside the house it was a little better. There were lots of rooms, four of them upstairs. Most of the rooms had old linoleum on the floors, and the kids had scrounged odds and ends of furniture, a lot of which was ripped, broken, or had parts missing. A couch was propped up on bricks at one end. Two big living room chairs sagged against the wall, one without a cushion.

One thing that I enjoyed was the candles. There must have been at least a hundred candles of every imaginable shape, size and color in the house. It wasn't the most effective source of light, but the candles were pretty in the evenings.

They did have running water. Danny explained to me that one of the boys had "found" the special tool required, and had simply gone out and turned the city water on himself. So far, the water plant hadn't noticed that someone was using the water without paying.

"What happens if you get caught?" I asked him.

"Nothing much," he said. "I guess they'd turn it off. Probably fix it so we couldn't turn it back on."

They were so casual about everything! I never did know for sure how many people stayed there, because as Danny had said, they came and went. But there were two girls, Susie and Carole, and at least six boys. Besides Danny, I more or less got to know Doug, Bob, Speed, and J.R. The sixth boy never talked and was seldom talked to by the others. When I wondered about that, Danny said it was just because the boy wanted it that way, and I never did know his name. There were others there for a day, or a night, or a few hours, but at least those eight were regularly there.

They made Sam and me welcome without making any kind of issue about it. It was just as Danny had said: I had provided some food, so it was okay for me to be there.

The only thing about our arrival that really got their attention was Sam; he was a hit from the moment we walked through the door.

Carole, a thin girl with pretty, natural blond curls and some bad acne scars, practically grabbed Sam right out of my arms. Sam didn't seem to mind. He liked the attention.

"Oh, what a beautiful little boy!" Carole cried, hugging Sam close as though he might have been her own long-lost child. "He looks a lot like Teddy," she said.

"Who's Teddy?" someone asked.

"My little brother, dummy," she replied. Then her expression saddened. "He looks like Teddy looked when I left home, I mean," she said. "I guess Teddy's a lot bigger now, though."

I wondered how long she'd been gone from home, why she had left, and where her hometown was. But I felt pretty certain that such questions wouldn't be appreciated, especially from a newcomer.

Danny had set the grocery bag on a rickety table in the kitchen, and a couple of the other boys began rummaging through the contents, helping themselves. I noticed that, although nobody there could be called a good housekeeper, the boys did sort of clean up after themselves.

When Sam began to get irritable and clearly ready for a nap, Carole said, "There's an extra mattress in room five. You and Sam can have it."

Room five? I went looking, and sure enough, someone had numbered all the bedrooms with a marking pen. The numbers were written on the door frames. Room five didn't have a door, just a makeshift curtain covering the opening. Not that it mattered to me at the moment, or the raggedy stained mattress on the floor either. It wasn't filthy, just old and shabby, and it looked to me like a grand bedroom. Until I saw that old mattress, I hadn't known that I was particularly tired.

I must have been thoroughly exhausted, for when I stretched out beside Sam, not intending to sleep but only to stay until he slept, I think my eyes closed almost before I had gotten comfortable. Two nights of sleeping on lumpy, scratchy hay, along with all the emotional strain, had worn me out a lot more than I'd realized.

When I awoke, it was late evening and Sam was gone. I leapt up and went searching for him. I needn't have worried.

Carole and Susie, along with Danny, Doug, and Speed, were entertaining Sam and being entertained by him. They had rigged a kind of high chair for him, and they were all seated around the table on boxes and chairs. Sam had made a fine mess with the Vienna sausage, crackers, and other goodies they had given him to eat. He was having a blast.

Susie, a tall, competent-looking, attractive girl who looked as though she didn't belong there, said, "We're glad you came, Marylou. Sam, here—he's just what we needed. He's just so *cute*!"

"He sure is," Doug agreed, grinning widely. "I never knew kids were so much fun."

"Haven't you ever been around little kids?" Danny asked him.

"Nope. Only seem 'em in grocery stores and laundries, mostly," he replied, "and they were always screaming or wetting their pants."

"Speaking of that," I began, going toward Sam, "I'd better take him . . ."

"We did that," Carole said. "Gee, Marylou, he's already potty trained! How'd you manage that? My mom never could get Teddy to . . ." Her voice trailed off, and she went to gaze out the window. She seemed so sad, suddenly, and I remembered another girl with a little butterfly cupped in her hands. It seemed there were all kinds of ways to be lonely.

The evening passed pleasantly, with everyone doing his own thing. The only thing that actually bothered me was that they played a radio *all* the time. At home, the radio was used only to hear weather forecasts and such, and I wasn't accustomed to such continuous noise. Before we went to sleep that night, I had begun to wish the batteries would run down.

But they probably had others. Batteries were small, and no doubt they were easy to slip into a pocket. . . .

That first afternoon and evening was wonderfully restful for me in most ways, though. Even in such a dilapidated place, with no way to cook real food even if anyone had wanted to, and only cold water, and candles for light, and too much noise, it did feel good to me to be with other young people. For some reason, I didn't feel the awful shyness that I'd always suffered from back home in school. And it felt good and comforting just not to be alone, to know there were people around me. And while I had always cared for Sam by myself without thinking of that responsibility as a burden, I discovered that it was nice to have someone else to wash his face or play with him sometimes. For a little while, I didn't even think about what I would do. I just relaxed and took it easy.

On Tuesday morning the boys all disappeared early, and just before noon, Carole put on makeup and a dress and left the house, too. That left just Sam and me with Susie.

When I began cleaning the place up, Susie joined in, though she didn't do too much. She smoked one cigarette after another, and she was also a talker. She told me that she was nearly eighteen, and that she'd been on her own for two years. She didn't seem to want to say why.

In that two years, she had been from Chicago to California, and she'd also been south to the Mexican border in Texas, and north to Detroit.

"I hate that place though," she said. "I'll never go back to Detroit. It's too rough there. You practically have to have a gun to survive."

I shuddered. "How have you managed?" I asked her. "Didn't you have trouble finding jobs?"

She blew out a thin stream of smoke and watched me for a moment through narrowed eyes. Then she spoke. "A girl can always earn a few bucks," she said, "and I've waitressed and done a few other things too. I even worked on a city street-cleaning crew for a while."

"What about the future?" I asked her. "Surely you plan to settle down sometime?"

"Oh sure," she agreed. Then a dreamy look appeared. "I'm sticking here for another week or two, kind of getting myself together. Then I'm headed for Nashville. I figure I can get a record cut pretty easily. I sing real good. J.R. says I sound just like Loretta Lynn."

"But I'll bet Loretta Lynn doesn't . . ." I shut up.

"Doesn't what?" Susie asked.

"Oh nothing," I said. "I forgot what I was going to say."

I hadn't forgotten though. I had started to say I didn't think a successful country music star puffed on cigarettes all day, but Susie was older and a lot more experienced than I, so I kept quiet.

That evening passed much as the preceding one had done,

except that Danny wasn't around. And during the night, I heard more than one person come in, and someone left.

On the following morning I walked in on Carole and Susie in the middle of an argument. I listened, curious about what their difference of opinion was. They faced one another in the living room, and Carole looked pathetic.

"It's your *turn*, that's all I'm saying," Carole insisted.

"It is not," Susie replied firmly. "I know you worked yesterday, but last week I went on Thursday and Friday both, while you stayed here. So it's your turn. You owe me a day."

"But that was because I was feeling so bad," Carole said. "It shouldn't count when one of us is sick."

"You like to eat, same as the rest of us," Susie replied. Her voice had grown angry and her eyes narrowed. "I was here first. When you came, you agreed to take turns. Now you're trying to chicken out, and it won't work!"

Carole's shoulders slumped, and she looked even more miserable. "All right," she said. "I'll go. I don't mean to take advantage, but you just can't imagine how much I hate it. Those crummy, lousy men, treating me like a piece of trash they've bought . . ." Her voice trailed off then, when she saw me in the doorway.

Maybe my mouth had fallen open when I'd finally understood. I know I felt sick to my stomach. "Everybody helps, any way they can," Danny had said. Would they expect me to "help," too—in the same way?

I went into the kitchen, and Danny was sitting at the table drinking a warm soda. I was embarrassed to look at him, but he didn't seem to notice.

"Sleep well?" he asked, glancing at me.

"Yes, just fine, thank you," I said. Then, because I didn't know what else to say, I said, "What are you going to do today?"

"Go out for a while I guess. See if I can pick up anything," he said. "I was supposed to bag groceries today, but Doug went in my place."

I wondered if he meant the same kind of "picking up" that he'd done the day I'd met him. He did.

"You ought to go along," he said. "It's easier if there's two. Especially if we took Sam. I'll bet I could carry off half of J.C. Penney's if we had Sam along. They won't pay much attention to a couple with a kid."

It made me sick. But he sounded so awfully bitter, so sarcastic, and I remembered him saying that he didn't like to steal. In spite of my disgust, I felt a little bit sorry for him.

"Are you saying that I have to—that I really *should* go?" I asked him.

He nodded, not looking at me. "You wouldn't get kicked out for a few more days even if you didn't help," he said, "but pretty soon they'll start putting the pressure on. And I think you'd like helping me better than . . . I mean, the way the girls usually get money is . . ."

"I know," I said quickly.

"Look, Marylou," he said then, "I didn't really want to bring you here. I mean, I could tell you're not exactly used to living like this. But I was pretty sure you wouldn't have really gone home that day, and I was afraid you'd get into real trouble on your own. But now, if you've had a chance to think it over . . . maybe you do want to go back now? If you do, I'll help you, go to the cops with you or whatever."

Under the circumstances, I felt he was making a generous offer. Yet I still couldn't decide. Although I was getting pretty uncomfortable there, I just didn't feel able to make the decision that would condemn Sam to Uncle Ed's hatred—or myself to being alone and unloved again, like I'd been before I got Sam.

"I've been avoiding thinking about it, to tell you the truth," I said. "Danny . . . let me stay here today, and I'll make up my mind. If I decide to stay here, I'll go and . . . and help you tomorrow. I promise."

He nodded, and sat looking into his soda can as if there was something there he needed to see.

"Danny . . ." I began hesitantly.

"Yeah?"

"I guess I'm not supposed to ask this kind of question,"

I said, "but . . . why are *you* living like this? Surely you had a home somewhere, a family. Why did you leave?"

I will never forget the way his eyes clouded and grew distant, the feeling of utter helplessness so thick around him that it was almost visible. He didn't answer me for a while. And when he did, I wished I hadn't asked.

"Keep whatever illusions you've got left about the goodness of human nature, Marylou," he said. "Take my word for it; you don't really want to know why I left home."

Then he got up and walked out into the yard, and he walked like a ninety-year-old man.

Chapter Seven

I HAD A lot to think about, and pretty soon I would have to make a decision. It had been easy to float along there with Danny and the others, putting off my worries about what I was going to do. But it couldn't go on much longer, and it was only fair. If I stayed, I owed it to them to help to pay our way, Sam's and mine. If I left, well, the options were pretty slim that way, too.

Danny left the house after a while, his shoulders slumped, and I couldn't help worrying about him getting arrested for stealing. Not that he didn't deserve getting caught, but just the same I didn't want it to happen.

He was moody and often bitter, but something about Danny drew me, his kindness I supposed. I still didn't know just how old he was, but it seemed to me that he was quite a lot more mature than the others who stayed there. I didn't know much about any of them of course, but I felt that the other boys, excepting the one who didn't talk, were a great deal alike in their casual, carefree attitudes. They acted as if nothing much mattered to them. They all enjoyed playing with Sam when he was feeling good and responding to them, but when he grew tired or fussy, Danny was the only one of the boys who showed patience and concern. I'd never really thought about that before, how the way someone reacts to a child could indicate so much about what they were like inside.

As for the girls, I simply didn't understand either of them.

Carole, so lonely and so taken with Sam because he reminded her of her own little brother, obviously hated what she was doing to earn her keep. Yet she kept on. Why? Surely Carole could find a better way to live if she simply couldn't go back home, whatever or wherever "home" was. There were places where teenage girls could live and go to school and have more or less normal lives, weren't there?

But perhaps not, I realized, thinking it over. I felt certain that a quiet, almost shy girl like Carole couldn't have committed any crime that would make her afraid to ask for help. Still, who knew? Maybe if she did, say, call one of those hotlines for runaway kids, maybe they would just send her back to wherever she had come from. And maybe that would be worse than what she was doing now.

Then too, maybe she *had* done something so terrible that she was afraid to talk to any adults. . . . I had, hadn't I?

But that's different, another part of my mind argued. I hadn't *meant* to commit a crime. I had only wanted to protect Sam. If I just hadn't let it get out of control . . . but I had.

Susie was completely different from Carole. Susie didn't show any signs of regret or give any indication that she was lonely or missing any family or anything. I liked her, sort of, but thoughts of Susie didn't arouse the same feelings of pity I had for Carole. Susie was one who would survive. She wasn't very realistic, but it was plain enough that one way or another she would take care of herself. To Susie, as to the boys except for Danny, Sam was a toy, fun when he was clean and cute and playful, and a nuisance when he wasn't.

Could Sam and I stay? Could I "help" Danny and pay our way? I didn't think so. Aside from the shoplifting that I knew I would never be able to do, I thought that I might be able to find some kind of job and support us honestly. I wouldn't have to earn a lot, since the only expense at that house was for food—but who would care for Sam? Oh, I felt sure the others would be willing to take turns looking after him, but was I willing to do it that way?

None of them would actually mistreat Sam. It was more the other way around; already they were spoiling him, giving in to his every wish. But they were just too casual to be trusted to watch him carefully enough; they weren't accustomed to it. And I would have no right to complain, either. Sam was *my* responsibility, and I already knew well enough how only a minute's forgetfulness could result in his being hurt.

We couldn't stay there.

Recognizing how impossible it was for us to stay made me sad. It was a peculiar and aching thing, and in some odd way it was a shameful thing to face, knowing that in those few days with a bunch of runaway kids who supported themselves mostly by prostitution and stealing, I had felt more real kinship, more a part of a family, than I'd felt for years with Uncle Ed and Aunt Bonnie.

"Why couldn't you have loved Sam and me a little bit?" I screamed at them silently while I washed our few clothes and prepared for us to leave. If only they had shown some affection now and then, the blows from Uncle Ed's too-eager hands would not have hurt nearly so much. If only Uncle Ed hadn't kept saying and doing things to show how he despised Sam for his mixed blood, I wouldn't have been nearly so afraid of going off to school and leaving Sam with them. If only Mr. Patterson had listened to me and at least considered that he might have made a mistake in placing Sam. . . .

But "if only" wouldn't solve any of our problems.

Washing our clothes by hand in cold water didn't produce the very best results, but they smelled clean at least. The weather was hot, although in the few days since I'd left home, the real heat wave had apparently passed. Anyhow, our clothes dried in a little while after I draped them over the makeshift clothesline, and I smoothed them out as well as I could and packed all but a change each into the backpack again. By the time I had finished, it was the middle of the afternoon, and I began to get seriously worried about Danny. He'd been gone an awfully long time. I couldn't leave without at least telling him good-bye. Danny had been nice to Sam and me.

He finally returned around five o'clock, and he didn't bring any food at all. I wondered about that, but it wasn't any of my business what he'd been doing all day.

I did want to talk to Danny though, and when I saw him going out the front door while the others were arguing over a card game, I picked Sam up and followed him. He was sitting on the sagging steps, staring into space.

"Danny, can I talk to you for a minute?" I asked.

He moved over, giving me room to join him without saying anything. I sat, and Sam started scrambling out of my lap toward Danny.

"Sam, be still," I said.

"It's okay," Danny mumbled, encircling Sam with one arm and drawing him close. Sam snuggled against him contentedly.

Then I couldn't think what I wanted to say, so we just sat there without talking for a while. The sun had sunk below the rooftops, and it was pleasant and almost cool sitting there. But I had to say something, so finally I just said, "Thank you for being so nice to us, Danny. For bringing us here and everything, I mean."

"I'm not too sure I did you any favors," he replied quietly. "This ain't exactly the best place for you and Sam to be, you know."

"I guess not," I said, "but it's been a big help just the same. And besides, I've sort of liked it. I've felt like I had . . . well, friends, you know?"

He looked at me for a while, and I didn't think he seemed too pleased. I wondered if I'd said something wrong.

"So you've decided to stay," he said in a flat voice.

"What if I have?" I asked, puzzled by his attitude. "Would you like that, or . . . or not?" Then I felt myself blushing, and I looked away from his troubling eyes.

"Do whatever you want," he said after a moment, in that same uninterested way. "I'm nobody to tell you what to do."

I looked back at him, but he had turned his face away. I felt hurt by his lack of concern, and even as I recognized my own hurt, I knew it was foolish. I'd known him for a few days, barely talked to him, and didn't really know anything about him. I had no right to expect Danny to care about me or Sam either. He had plenty of problems of his own, I was sure.

And yet I couldn't help noticing how gently he handled Sam, who had started climbing all over him. Danny's hands went so naturally and gently to support Sam, to keep him from falling. He did it without thinking about it. I thought it unlikely that Danny had ever had much to do with little kids, but caring for Sam seemed to come so naturally to him.

I swallowed the hurt and answered. "No," I said. "We're not going to stay here. We're going to leave in the morning."

Then Danny wanted to know why I'd decided to leave!

So I told him. "Whatever I do, it has to be for Sam's good," I said, "and I don't think that staying here is the right thing for him."

"Why not?" Danny asked. He still wasn't looking at me.

"Well," I began, unsure how to explain, "I guess maybe it'll sound kind of silly. I mean, I'm not even quite sixteen yet. But I've got to sort of . . . do whatever is good for Sam's *future*, see? He has to be loved and taken care of while he's little, and maybe he would get that here. It's better than living back home, at least that way. But the kids here . . . there just isn't any future for them, not the way they look at things. I mean, they love Sam and all, but Sam has to grow up, and be educated and learn how to make something out of his life someday, and . . ."

". . . and since the kids here haven't grown up yet themselves . . ." Danny interrupted, musing.

"Yeah, that's about it," I mumbled.

At last he turned toward me, shifting Sam to sit on his other knee. His eyes were friendly at last; the dull look had disappeared.

"You had me worried for a little while there, Marylou," he said, almost smiling. "I sure was afraid you'd decided to stay here."

"But you're the one who *brought* us here," I said, puzzled.

"Yeah, that's what was bothering me the most I guess,"

he said. "I didn't like thinking that I was gonna be the cause of you doing stuff that . . . that you don't have any business doing."

I puzzled over that for a while. What in the world was I to make of Danny? Was this his way of saying that he actually cared about Sam and me? And what if he did, what did I care? I had way too many things to worry about already. There wasn't any place or time for me to waste in thinking about such things. Besides, Danny was a runaway, too. There was no future for either Sam *or* me in thinking very much about *him*.

Chapter Eight

THAT NIGHT, WHEN a few hours' rest was so tremendously important to me, I could not sleep. It was long past midnight before my eyes finally closed. Until then, my thoughts jumped from one thing to another and I could make no sense of anything; at last I faced the problem squarely.

I had concluded that I had to leave. The question was, would I go back home?

I played a little "what if" game in my mind. What if I turned myself in, was there any chance that I *wouldn't* be sent to that correctional school? I didn't think so. I had kidnapped Sam, and we'd been away for about a week, and I hadn't even let anyone know that Sam and I were safe.

But I would. No matter what else happened, I would call Aunt Bonnie in the morning. No, I'd call the welfare office or the police station. Aunt Bonnie had watched Uncle Ed knock Sam around without a word of protest. She didn't care whether we were even alive or not—or at least she didn't care very much. I wouldn't call Aunt Bonnie, but I *would* call someone. It wouldn't make any difference in what happened to Sam and me, but it didn't seem fair, now that I was considering it, that the police might be spending their time looking for a real kidnapper, not when I was the only one to blame. I would just say that we were safe and well, and then hang up quickly.

Okay, so that much had been settled. No matter what else

happened, I would do that much in the morning. At last, I had made one decision!

What if I turned myself in; my own punishment aside, would I be able to make anyone listen to me and recognize that Sam *had* to be placed in a different home? Well . . . if I had gone back right away, there might have been a chance. But now that I had kept Sam away for so long, I doubted that any adult would be willing to give me credit for having enough sense to know what was right for Sam.

It was funny. When I thought of it like that, I couldn't find much reason to blame anyone for thinking I was an irresponsible and even dangerous person. How would *I* feel about some other kid who'd done what I had done, especially without having some solid evidence to suggest there was a reason for it? Uh-oh, that answered my questions all right! Even the *truth* wasn't going to be enough of a defense.

But what if we *could* go back to Uncle Ed and Aunt Bonnie's; just go back to the way things were with nothing changed? If we could do that, would I even want to?

It was an interesting question. I knew that I wouldn't have left in the first place if I hadn't been so upset. I would have stayed right there, at least for a while longer, and who could tell? Maybe I would have been able to have found a reasonable solution.

But I *had* run away with Sam. Furthermore, in the week since, bad as it had been in some ways, I had felt that a few people liked me, and loved Sam. Nobody had hit me; nobody had hit Sam. Nobody had even yelled at either of us.

No, even if I could go back without recriminations, I wouldn't want to, for myself or for Sam. I knew that by the end of the following day, we might very well *be* back there, but if it happened that way, it certainly would be only because I'd had no other choice. There was nothing there for us except shelter, a skimpy diet, and yard-sale clothing. I supposed that to some folks that would sound wonderful, but I still wanted something more for both of us. I wanted safety, and I even dared to want a little bit of love.

* * *

It took a long time for me to wake up and get moving the next morning. Sam even slept late for a change, and I expected the house might be empty except for the two of us, when we were up and dressed at last.

It wasn't though. Not quite. When I walked into the kitchen, there sat Danny, his hands cupped around a soda can. It was so exactly as I'd seen him the day before, and I was still groggy from sleep. For a moment I felt disoriented; was this some freaky sort of replay of what had already happened once?

But Danny looked up at us and smiled, the first complete, honest-to-goodness smile I'd ever seen on his face. It was as if a light had clicked on inside his head. His eyes weren't nearly so dark and brooding. Smiling, Danny was positively handsome!

"Good morning," he said. "I thought you two were never gonna wake up! C'mere, Sam. Want a drink?"

Sam reached for him eagerly, and I knew I should protest his giving Sam a drink of soda first thing in the morning, but I didn't. One way or another this wasn't going to be an ordinary day; might as well relax while I could!

We had a little breakfast then. It was almost a normal meal, because Danny had gone out and bought a box of dry cereal and a quart of milk. It was delicious! Sam gulped the cold milk as if he was starving, and I cringed with guilt. Little kids were supposed to have fresh milk every day, and this was the first Sam had had in several days. I certainly wasn't providing for him very well.

Then I reminded myself that lots of times there had been no milk at Uncle Ed's either. Near the end of the month when their money had about run out, we had done without lots of things most folks consider essential. When it was a question of buying milk or beer, there hadn't ever been any real question at all. The money went for beer.

I made that breakfast scene last as long as I could stretch it out, because I dreaded walking away from that house. Whatever else it was, the place had provided shelter and food and carefree acceptance. I hated the thought of leaving that bit of security.

I hated the thought of leaving Danny, too, but I tried to ignore those feelings. I felt sure that he too was doing a bit of acting, that he sensed my reluctance and my fear, but at last he asked the question.

"Have you decided what you're going to do now, Marylou?"

"Yes," I replied, dispirited. "For one thing, I'm going to call the sheriff's office back home and tell them that Sam and I are all right."

Danny nodded. "That makes sense," he said. Then, "You're not calling your aunt and uncle?"

"The sheriff can tell them if he wants to," I muttered.

"Okay, so you're going to call someone," he said. "Then what?"

At first I wasn't going to tell him about the second decision I had made during the night. Then I changed my mind. Danny deserved to know, I thought. More important, he *wanted* to know, because he really did care.

I paced the kitchen floor while I explained. "I hope you aren't going to think I'm completely crazy," I said, "but here's what I've decided. I don't think I ever had any choice, really. I just didn't want to admit it.

"I can't provide for Sam. There's just too many odds against it. I'm not old enough to have a decent job, and even if I was older, it still wouldn't work because nobody can make a real future for a little kid, without an education. I'm just not smart enough. So I'm going back. I *want* Sam to be mine, but the truth is, he *isn't* mine. I have to take him back."

Danny's face clouded, but he nodded his head. "It scares me a lot, what might happen to you and Sam both," he said, "but it looks like you're right. I mean, it's not *right*, but at least there's a chance you'll both be okay. Here, with no way to get by except . . . and at least when you go back they *might* listen to you and see that Sam . . . that Sam has someone who'll . . . love him."

Danny was almost crying, I thought, and that brought tears to my own eyes. I had managed not to cry until then, but I had to swallow hard to keep from breaking down when I recognized the threat of tears in Danny's voice. We were quiet for a little while, then Danny said in a more normal voice, "If you're going back, why are you going to call the sheriff? I mean, are you going to tell him, ask him to come and get you or something?"

I shook my head, dreading to say the rest, but knowing I would have to tell him.

"No," I said. "I'm not going to ask him to come for us, because I'm not going back for a little while longer."

His eyes widened. "You're going to stay here?" he asked.

Again I shook my head. "Remember the place I told you about?" I asked. "The barn where Sam and I stayed for two nights? I'm going to spend the rest of my money, or almost all the rest, on food, and Sam and I are going to stay in that barn until the food's gone. *Then* we're going back."

"But that's *crazy*, Marylou!" Danny yelled, startling Sam, who stared up at Danny with wide, frightened eyes. Seeing Sam's expression, Danny quickly hugged him close, while he glared at me. "That's the nuttiest thing I ever heard," he said to me in a calmer tone. "It's dangerous. Anything could happen to you! Why not just stay here a few more days?"

"Because," I said firmly, "I know that I'm going to lose Sam the minute we go back. And before I do, I want a couple of days with him, just the two of us. I want to . . . I want to . . . to *save up* some things about Sam, to *absorb* . . . so I won't forget . . ."

I couldn't say any more, because my throat had closed up and my insides were twisting in a knot of pain. Then my whole body began to tremble, and the tears came. I couldn't help it; the sobs tore me apart and I fumbled for a chair and fell into it, blinded and aching with a heartache more agonizing than I had ever known that anyone could feel.

Chapter Nine

POOR DANNY! HE had his hands full for a little while, because my crying got Sam upset and he started crying, too. And there Danny was, trying and failing to quiet Sam, then trying to get me to stop crying so Sam would settle down.

We both quieted after a little while, and I was finally able to explain to Danny that the barn was quite safe, that the house was deserted, and it was all at the end of a dead-end road, so there wouldn't even be any traffic out there.

"You said the barn's full of hay," Danny said. "What'll you do if whoever owns it comes and finds you and Sam there?"

"I thought of that," I told him. "If that happens, I'll just tell the truth, probably even ask for a ride to the nearest telephone and let the guy hear me turn myself in. After all, a farmer ought to be someone I could trust, and we aren't going to damage anything, just sleeping on his hay. Danny, I wouldn't even think of going back there if I didn't feel really sure. Nobody but you will ever know we were there, and I just have to have a little more time with Sam."

"Well, all right," he said at last. "I won't argue with you any more. There's just one thing. I'm walking out there with you."

"That'll be nice," I said happily. "The only thing that bothers me at all is walking out there by myself. So if you come along, I won't even have that to worry about."

"We'd better get going then," Danny said, "because I've got to be back in town by three o'clock."

"What for?" I asked.

"Tell you later," he said. He was smiling again.

It was the nicest walk of my whole life, I think. It wasn't too hot, and a cheery breeze teased at my hair. Danny carried Sam until we came to a little house with a fenced yard. He put Sam down and leaned against the gate, looking at the house. I wondered what he was up to. A FOR RENT sign hung on the front door.

"I've noticed this place," Danny said. "What do you think, Marylou? Wouldn't this be a neat place to live?"

"Oh yes," I agreed. "It's a cute place all right. Not very big, but it looks solid and clean."

"Good yard, too," he murmured. "It'd be a great yard for a kid, fenced in and everything."

"Probably expensive to rent," I said.

"Oh, I don't know, maybe not," Danny said. "Well, I guess we'd better get on."

So we walked on, not stopping again until we came to the little store where Danny and I had met that first day. We went inside, and I got change for the pay phone. Then I got the number of the sheriff's office back home. Danny held Sam while I dialed the number.

I heard the sound of the receiver being lifted, then a voice. "Sheriff's office, Deputy Stone speaking."

I swallowed hard. I knew Randy Stone. He was only about twenty or so. He lived near Uncle Ed and Aunt Bonnie.

"Randy, this is Marylou Britten," I said. "I just wanted someone to know that Sam and I are fine, and that nobody kidnapped us or anything."

"Marylou!" he gasped, "Where *are* you?"

"Not too far away," I said. "In a few days Sam and I will be back. We'll probably come to your office."

"Marylou, don't hang . . ."

But I hung up. Randy Stone was a pretty nice guy. I couldn't talk to him anymore; he'd talk me into telling him everything, and I wasn't quite ready yet.

With Danny's help, I bought food that wouldn't spoil very quickly, much the same things as we'd been eating at the house, and I filled the same orange-juice jug with water. That gave us a bit more to carry, but it wasn't too far to the edge of town and the gravel road leading to our barn.

The place was as deserted as when I'd been there before, and when Danny had looked around some, he seemed more at ease about the whole thing. I put Sam down for a nap then, and Danny and I sat and leaned back against the stacked hay. His usual brooding and troubled expression had returned, and I figured he was worrying again about Sam and me.

I guess he was, but there was more.

"Marylou, I want to ask a favor," he finally said. He sounded as if he was almost afraid.

"Of course, Danny," I said. "What is it?"

"You've got to know how important it is to me," he said, speaking slowly, reluctantly. "What I want you to do is to promise me something . . . that no matter what happens to you and Sam after you leave here, that you'll write to me, regular. I'll . . . I'll have an address, I'm almost sure."

"Of course I will," I promised quickly, pleased that he wanted to keep in touch. I felt warm all over, just knowing that. And he considered it a *favor*?

"That little house I showed you . . . I'm going to rent it in two more weeks," he said. My mouth fell open and I started to ask questions, but he went on, talking fast then.

"I already talked to the owner. The rent's cheap enough, and there's even some furniture in it I can use. Marylou, yesterday I got a job! I start today at three o'clock, and in two weeks I'll get my first paycheck."

I was amazed and thrilled, and I could see that my pleasure made Danny feel even better. He told me about the job; it was in a place where they made parts for household appliances; not a big place, but it had been in business for years. At first his pay would be just a little bit over minimum wage, but in just six weeks he would get his first raise.

"The guy's taking a chance on me," Danny said. "I told

him the truth about myself, or a lot of it anyhow, and he didn't say anything except, 'You're through being a bum, then?' And when I said yes, he said, 'Be here at three o'clock tomorrow afternoon, ready to work.' I couldn't believe it, Marylou! Everywhere I've tried to get a job, they either say they don't hire seventeen-year-olds, or they get all uptight about me not having any education, or because I don't have any references, or something. This will be the first real job I've ever had except for temporary things like bagging groceries or fixing flats. I'm going to do *good* for that guy, Marylou. I'm going to work so hard . . .'' His voice trailed off and he looked away. I figured he was embarrassed about showing me so much of his feelings.

"I'm real glad, Danny," I said. "I'll bet you'll get to be a foreman or something before long, because you're smart, whether you've got any education or not, and I know you'll work hard."

"I thought about . . . about trying to get you to stay back at the house for the two weeks," Danny said softly, still not looking at me. "I thought about you and me and Sam living in that little house after I got paid."

My heart leaped and turned over, I think. Oh, I liked Danny a lot, and it was so good, good, *good* to be wanted!

He turned to face me then, and his face was flushed. "I didn't mean anything bad by that," he said. "I just thought that I'd like to take care of you and Sam. But even two more weeks back at the house is too long. And besides, what if we got found out? We probably would, sooner or later, and then they'd take Sam away and probably put us both in jail for twenty years. Then I knew that it was a dumb idea. You really do have to take Sam back."

I nodded. "I know," I said, "but . . . thanks for wanting us, Danny. It sure means a lot to me, and I kind of wish we could . . . but you'll do really fine by yourself anyway. And I *will* write to you, no matter what—if they let people write letters from reform school, that is."

"They do," Danny said. "I never wrote any letters because I didn't have anyone to write to, but the other boys did."

"*You* were in reform school?" I asked, amazed.

He nodded. "They couldn't find a foster home for me right away, and all the kids' homes were full or something. Anyway, they put me in the reform school for a while. Then they took me out and sent me to this foster home. It was okay, but I was all messed up and didn't have sense enough to know when I was well off. I ran away."

"But why did . . ."

"I'll tell you a little. Maybe it'll make sense to you some way. It's mostly to let you know why it's so important to me for you to write me letters," he said, talking fast. "I don't have anybody, Marylou, and I want to—to make something good out of my life, like you said yesterday about Sam. I'm afraid I'll never make it unless there's somebody who gives a hoot whether I do okay or not."

Then he told me more. Danny's father was in a state penitentiary and would be for many more years. He was there for committing kinds of abuse against Danny, his own son, that make me sick and ashamed to think about. But I couldn't tell it if I wanted to, because I promised not to ever tell it. His mother had died of a heart attack during his father's trial. When he ran away from the foster home, he was barely thirteen. He had been on his own ever since, for four years.

Danny didn't tell a lot of details; he just skimmed over the story, so to speak. I was glad. I don't think I could have endured hearing much more. As it was, I felt almost ashamed of thinking I'd had a hard time. Even Uncle Ed's knocking Sam and me around didn't seem nearly so terrible anymore, and I told Danny that.

Danny didn't agree; in fact, he almost got angry. "You were right to feel that this Uncle Ed was a bas . . . a good-for-nothing bully," he said, "and you're right when you say they should never put any more kids in that home. Sure, you and Sam didn't get really *hurt*, but that's because you just up and left there to protect Sam. Don't you *ever* feel bad about that, Marylou. Maybe you didn't do exactly the best thing, but you did what you thought was right at the time, and you did it for the right reasons."

"Okay, I'll try to keep thinking of it like that," I said. "If I can do it, at least it'll make *me* feel better."

"Think about it like this, then," Danny said. "Think about how much better I might be right now if somebody'd tried to protect *me*."

"I think you're pretty doggone good anyway, Danny," I whispered. "I think you've got more courage than anybody I've ever heard of!"

Danny left a few minutes later. Maybe I only imagined it, but it did seem as if he even walked differently than I'd seen him do before. It seemed like he was eager to get somewhere, and like he suddenly weighed about a hundred pounds less.

I looked at our food and tried to figure out how long it would last. I thought it would probably last for two more days. Sam and I would be able to stay at least two nights. Then we'd have to go.

I sat thinking about everything that had happened since I left home, but not worrying about any of it really, just passing the time while Sam slept. I had made up my mind about one thing, for sure and certain. I wasn't going to let *anything* take my attention from Sam for the next couple of days. I was going to talk to him and play with him and try to remember every single detail, so I would have a lot of good things to think about while I . . . when whatever was going to happen to me had happened. And maybe, just maybe, Sam would remember, too. . . .

The only interruption we would have would be Danny's visit the next day before he went to work. "If I come out here one day and you and Sam are gone, I'm going to figure that you've gone home," he said. Then he handed me a slip of paper. "This is the address of the little house," he said. "I'll be living there two weeks from today. I'll expect to wake up sometime in the two or three days after that, and find a letter from you in my mailbox."

"It'll be there, Danny," I promised. "If I'm alive and not

66

too far back in prison, there'll be a letter in two and a half weeks.''

It was a simple thing I had vowed to do. Promises are easy enough to make, and jokes too, like ''if I'm alive . . .'' But sometimes promises are broken, and jokes can turn out to be much too close to reality.

Chapter Ten

SAM AND I played that afternoon. I helped him climb on the stacked hay for a while, and then I dragged a few of the bales around until I had made a kind of tunnel, only without a roof. Sam loved it. He'd go running between the walls of stacked hay, calling out, "Ma'Lou not catch Sam! Sam run *fast*. Ma'Lou not catch Sam!" But of course he wanted me to do just that, and when I caught him, lifting him high into the air, he erupted into joyful giggles and squeals.

Oh, he was beautiful, not just in his appearance but in his very spirit. He was such a happy little boy, so easily entertained and pleased! Everything interested him. He would study a curled leaf or a bug or an intricately formed pebble for the longest time. I hadn't known that little kids could be so attentive, and of course I thought Sam was very special. To me he was more beautiful than other children, and certainly far beyond average in intelligence! I loved him so, because he was my own baby brother—only he really wasn't.

But I refused to brood about anything. Our time alone was to be a happy time, a bit of perfection that I would keep with me always in memory. When the fears of what was to happen threatened to settle on my mind like an infection of spirit, I mentally pushed them away. For Sam and me the clock and calendar had stopped. Like the worries, they would not be permitted to resume until we ran out of food.

We rested well that night. Nothing disturbed us, and when morning came it was a bright and beautiful day. Our breakfast consisted of cheese and crackers, apples, and canned juiced. We made it last for a long time with games and giggles and fun and hugs.

I decided that hiding out inside the barn really wasn't necessary any longer, so when we had finished our meal, washed up a bit, and done the best we could do with a comb and wrinkled but clean clothes, we went outside. For a long while I stood gazing at the little rundown house a few yards away, with the high-pitched roof and newsprint windows. I wanted to go exploring. Would the doors be locked? Maybe someone used the house for storage, or maybe it would contain only mice and a few broken dishes left by the latest occupant. It would be fun to explore.

Yet my feet seemed to object. When I started to walk toward the house, something almost tugged at me, and soon Sam and I were walking in the opposite direction, up the lane and toward the highway. "Chicken!" I scolded myself. But the house wasn't mine; it was bad enough that we were trespassing in the barn. Besides, what if Danny came and we missed him?

We'd barely started back up the road when Sam remembered his entertainment of a few days before. "G'ashoppers!" he cried. "Sam get g'ashoppers!" And off he went, running as fast as his little legs could go in a fruitless effort to catch one of the quick little creatures. It didn't seem to bother him that they were too fast, that he didn't come close to catching one. He was always persistent.

I remembered one morning not long after he came. Sam was sitting on the floor playing with a plastic toy shaped like a bowling pin. I called to him, and he got to his feet. In the process he knocked the bowling pin down. He sat back down, righted the bowling pin, then got up, knocking it over again. And again he sat down to set the thing in an upright position. Over and over he went through the same motions, until at last he managed to get to his feet without bumping the bowling pin.

I'd been so amazed that day, recognizing Sam's remarkable determination. With such persistence apparently born in him, Sam was sure to accomplish great things some day if he could be raised with love and security. He had none of the terrible shyness that had plagued me throughout my childhood, and with all my heart I wanted him to always be as warm and loving and outgoing as he was then.

I walked along slowly, aware of Sam of course, but lost in memories nevertheless. We were moving slowly, taking our time because we weren't going anywhere anyway, and I wasn't conscious of anything much except in the part of my mind that stayed alert to Sam. The sun was warm, just enough to feel good, and a light breeze came from somewhere. I could smell the lovely, light aroma of the honeysuckle that massed on an old rundown fence beside the road. It was a most beautiful, happy day.

I became aware that Sam had grown quiet, and when I looked down at him, he was standing perfectly still, gazing ahead. Then he burst into laughter, and with his little body practically dancing its delight, he pointed. "Dan-nee!" he cried happily. "Ma'Lou see. Dan-nee!"

I looked ahead then, and sure enough it was Danny coming toward us. Even from the distance I could see that he was smiling, and that his walk was jaunty and energetic, not heavy and tired-looking as it had been before. Quickly he reached us, and he lifted Sam high, making him chuckle and kick, then he hugged him close. Sam clung to him for a couple of seconds, then began wiggling around, wanting down to play again.

Danny set him gently down, and Sam immediately took off again. This time he cried, "Dan-nee see! Sam catch g'ashoppers!"

I could barely recognize Danny's face, so different than before. His eyes danced, and there seemed to be a kind of glow about him. Evidently his first day on the new job had gone well, but could such a thing bring *that* much pleasure into his face?

He had hardly looked at me; he watched Sam's every move, and then he said, "Sam said my name, Marylou! He's calling me Danny!"

70

Then I understood. While we'd been at the house those few days, Sam had been quick to pick up the names of the kids who lived there. First he had learned Carole's name, but by the next afternoon he had easily said the names of the others: Doug, Susie, J.R. . . . all of them in fact, except Danny's. When I had tried to get him to say "Danny," surely not a difficult name for him to pronounce, Sam had simply not responded.

I was touched to see how deeply such a simple thing as Sam's saying his name pleased Danny. How awfully lonely Danny must have been feeling all those years, to be so affected by hearing Sam call out to him!

Danny simply joined us on our walk, turning with us to go in the direction from which he had just come, away from our barn. We watched as Sam carefully filled his little pockets with selected rocks and such. The pocket on his right side was easy, but being right-handed, he tried for a long time to reach across with that hand to fill the left-hand pocket. It was comical to watch him twist and turn, moving his whole body and getting nowhere.

"Like a cat chasing its tail," Danny whispered, smiling.

He dropped nearly everything in his effort, and just when I was about to help him, he began to transfer his treasures to his left hand, then use that hand to fill his pocket.

"He sure is a smart little guy," Danny observed.

I nodded my agreement. "It takes awhile, but he does usually manage to figure things out for himself," I said. "I helped him to do everything at first, till I finally realized that he wouldn't learn if I did it all for him." Then I asked, "How did the job go, Danny?"

That triggered an absolute flood! Danny, who so often mumbled half sentences in reluctant answers to questions, began to talk rapidly, his words tumbling over themselves in his eagerness to express his happiness.

"It was terrific!" he exclaimed. "The boss taught me himself, and the other guys told me at break time that he never does that, that he always has one of the foremen to break in a new employee. I wonder why *he* decided to teach

71

me. . . . anyway, I'm operating this machine, and it's pretty complicated, only not *too* much, and it's all controlled by this computer, see? And what I have to do is to keep a real close eye on the machine, and when one batch of parts is finished, I have to—uh—tell the computer to change the machine over, to get ready to operate differently, for a different kind of part, and it's really interesting and even fun to do, and the boss—he's Mr. Scofield—he said that I learned how to do it faster than anybody has ever learned before, and . . ."

On and on he went, explaining the process in detail, much of which I didn't even begin to understand. It was wonderful though, to listen to Danny, to see his enthusiasm and especially to hear the note of real *pride* in his voice.

It was a new experience for me, too, because I'd never had occasion to think about how much having a job with an apparent future could mean to a person.

At last he sort of ran down, and he said sheepishly, "I guess I've really been running on, huh? Probably boring you to death."

"Oh no," I said, "It's interesting, and I'm so glad that you like the job and the boss likes you and all that."

"Yeah, it's a real break," Danny said. "I still can't believe it. I had about given up on ever being able to support myself—honestly, I mean. I almost didn't even go in there the other day to ask for a job. To tell you the truth, I was even kinda scared."

"Scared?" I asked. "Why scared?"

"I don't know. Of being turned down again I guess. But then I knew I just *had* to do it, scared or not. So I did, and I sure am glad."

"Me too," I said. "How come you thought you *had* to try on that particular day?" I asked.

"It was mostly on account of you, Marylou," Danny replied, quiet but sure of himself. "It was the look on your face that first day when I took . . . when I stole the stuff from those stores. You didn't say anything, but I was ashamed, just seeing the look on your face."

72

My own face flushed just hearing him, but I was glad if my surprise at his stealing had affected him that way. I thought how funny it was that a person maybe *thinks* he knows how he's affecting other people, but he never really knows for sure. . . .

When we had almost reached the highway, we turned around and started back. In a little while Sam began to slow down. He was getting tired, and Danny picked him up and carried him. Before we had even reached the barn, Sam's eyes were closing, and I spread out a couple of shirts on the hay, and Danny laid him down gently. Sam's eyes fluttered open, and he smiled one sweet sleepy smile and murmured, "Dan-nee . . ."

As we had done on the previous day, Danny and I sat and talked while Sam slept, and after awhile, reluctantly, he asked me, "How much longer will you stay here, Marylou?"

"We'll have to leave in the morning I guess," I said. "I really do dread it, but . . . that's how it's got to be. But I'm glad that we came back here for a while first, Danny. It's been great, and I . . . and I'd better not talk about it anymore, or I'll be crying again."

"You haven't lost my address . . . the address of the little house, have you?" he asked.

"Not a chance," I said. "I've got the address memorized, but that piece of paper is my connection to the world, sort of. I'm keeping it with me, no matter what."

"Okay then," he said. "You'll be writing to me, so I'll know how you and Sam are doing. And after I've gotten a few paychecks, I'll be coming to visit you, wherever you are."

Then he said he had to leave because it was nearly noon, and he had to walk all the way back to the house to eat something and then walk to work.

"I'll be out here tomorrow morning and walk you and Sam into town, to . . . for you to call them," Danny said.

"Okay," I said, my chest aching with sadness. "If the farmer doesn't show up and run us off or something, I'll see you tomorrow morning."

73

We were standing then, and Danny's strong arms went around me and he drew me close to him. "Marylou, I love you," he whispered. "I don't know anything about being in love and all that, but I do know that I love you. You're my . . . my friend. Take care of yourself and Sam." Then he tipped my face up and wiped the tears from my eyes with a gentle finger, before he leaned close and touched his warm mouth to my trembling lips. And then he hurried away.

I could not remember ever having been kissed before in my whole life, except by Sam. I knew, as I stretched out on the hay beside Sam, that I shouldn't be thinking of Danny in a romantic kind of way. Neither of us had a very satisfactory past, and as for the future . . . there certainly wasn't any pot of gold that I could see, or for that matter, even a rainbow. But I did love Danny. Maybe it was like he had said, not the "in love" kind of love, but just the same it was love, and it felt more wonderful, more comforting than I had ever imagined in all my daydreams.

The rest of that fine and priceless day passed too quickly, and when darkness fell and Sam and I went back "to bed" for our last night in the barn, I couldn't sleep for a long time. At last I reached over and fished the paper with Danny's address out of the backpack, and holding it snug and safe in my hand gave me a kind of comfort. At last I slept.

I awakened abruptly soon afterward. Someone was shining a flashlight in my face, the glare and the shock blinding and confusing me. "Get up!" a harsh voice commanded. "Get up and get your things! You're not sneaking around in my barn any longer!"

Chapter Eleven

WITH THE LIGHT blinding me I couldn't see, but I got awkwardly to my feet, staggering with sleep and surprise. It was the middle of the night! What in the world was going on?

"Go on! Get your stuff and get out of here!" the voice said, and then I recognized that in spite of its harsh and grating quality, it was a woman's voice. I think I was a little less frightened then, but still scared to death.

"All right," I said. "I'll leave. I'm sorry. I didn't mean to be doing any harm. Sam and I just needed a place to sleep tonight. We were going to leave in the morning."

"Sam!" the voice practically screeched. "That boy who's been hanging around here? Where is he?"

Scared and terribly confused, it took a moment for me to understand, and also to realize that whoever this woman was, she had evidently been watching us since we'd come back to the barn.

"He's . . . he's not here," I explained nervously, cramming things into the backpack as fast as I could. "The boy who was here—he's in town, in Swifton. This is Sam."

I knelt down in the hay beside Sam. He had wiggled around in his sleep until his face was half covered by the shirt I had spread over him. When I drew the shirt away to put it into the pack with the rest of our things, the woman took a step forward, and I was aware that she had leaned forward to peer down at him.

"You've got a baby," she said. "I didn't know you had a baby. I don't see too well." Her voice had softened a bit, but it still sounded so strange, as if talking was an effort for her. She continued to look down at Sam while I eased the other cloth out from under him. I stuffed it into the pack and quickly slipped the pack on my back, then knelt again to pick Sam up. I lifted him carefully and he didn't awaken.

"We'll go now," I said, awake at last and not nearly so frightened as I'd been at first. "I'm sorry that we bothered you."

The woman stepped back, then followed us out of the barn. When I started for the road, she said, "Wait."

I stopped, and she approached close again. I still couldn't tell anything about her except that she was quite a bit taller than I.

"Come to the house," she said. "I didn't know you had a baby. Come to the house and sleep."

"Oh, no thank you," I said. "We were leaving in the morning anyway. Tonight will do just as well, and I don't want to bother you anymore."

She gestured toward the little house I'd been so curious about but never gone near. "It's too dark. You might fall and hurt the baby," she said.

"I'd really rather . . ." I began. She interrupted.

"Maybe you've been doing bad things," she said. "Maybe I should call the police. I might, if you don't come to the house so I can see what you're really like in the morning. And I don't want you to fall and hurt the baby."

I hesitated at that. This woman . . . there was something strange about her, and as for the things she'd said, I was having a hard time comprehending. It seemed that her words contained kind of . . . mixed messages.

Still, her distress at having tresspassers on her property was certainly understandable, especially since she was evidently a woman living alone. And what she'd had to say about Sam couldn't have been more sincere. It was clear that she was concerned with his safety.

Then there was the thing about the police to consider, too.

I truly did not want to be arrested, for trespassing *and* for kidnapping. It would be much better, I was sure, if I went back home on my own. I didn't want to sleep in this woman's house, but maybe it would be better to stay the rest of the night there. Maybe I could convince her that Sam and I meant no harm and hadn't done any damage. Then we could leave in the morning just as I had planned.

Again she gestured toward the house with the flashlight, and I said, "All right, we'll stay. Thank you."

There was no path from the barn to the house, and I walked through weeds, with the woman behind. With no hint of moonlight and no light coming from the house, it was difficult, and once I stumbled.

"Don't drop the baby," the woman said. Her flashlight wasn't much help to me. It seemed to me that she was shining it toward her own feet, and to my surprise she turned it off just before we reached the house.

"Go around to the other side," she said when I started toward the porch that I could barely see. I turned to the left and she followed. I could hear a faint jingling sound as she walked.

On the opposite side of the house from the barn there was another porch, and a door. The woman moved forward and pushed it open, and I stepped inside. It was pitch black.

"I suppose you'll need some light," she said flatly, and I heard the click of a switch. The room lightened, but not very much. It surely couldn't have been more than a twenty-five-watt bulb in the overhead light, and I couldn't begin to see into the corners of even that small room. It was a kitchen though; I could tell that much.

She opened a door to our right. More pitch darkness there.

"You'll sleep in here," she said, reaching around me to turn that light on. It too was unbelievably dim, but I could see a big bed and an old-fashioned dresser to one side.

"Do you want something to eat?" she asked then. "Is the baby hungry?"

"No thank you," I said. "Good night."

She didn't answer, but closed the bedroom door as she left

77

the room. The closing door made a loud click, and I wondered nervously if it had locked. But I was afraid to try it and see, and I didn't understand my fear. The woman was a little odd, not too talkative, but there'd been nothing about her to really frighten me.

I put Sam on the bed, and he squirmed around a bit, then with a deep sigh he settled back into a deep sleep. Next I put the backpack on the floor at the foot of the bed, and slipped my shoes off. Then, tiptoeing, I examined the room a little better.

It seemed to be clean, although I thought it was badly in need of airing. At the wall on what I thought was the south side, I discovered why.

There was a window, or rather, there had been one, I thought. On the inside, boards had been nailed over the opening, covering it completely so that not a speck of light could come through. Then I remembered the newsprint that I'd been able to see from the barn, and I wondered . . . was it possible that *all* the windows in this house were covered over? But surely not; that would be absolutely crazy!

But crazy or not, I was very tired and tomorrow was sure to be the most difficult day of my life. I needed desperately to sleep, and I turned out the pitiful light and crawled onto the bed beside Sam, snuggling close to him. We'd be leaving early, and the chances were that I would never get to sleep close to Sam again. With tears dripping onto my pillow, I drifted off to sleep for the second time that night.

Sam and I awoke at about the same time. I had no idea what time it was, because there was no way to see outside from that room. It was still so dark that I could barely see, and I turned the light on, which helped a little bit. In my bare feet I emptied my backpack onto the bed and got out our last clean clothes. We dressed, and I repacked everything.

It seemed that something was missing, and even after I realized that I'd left our water jug in the barn, I still felt that I didn't have everything. Then I knew what it was; the paper with Danny's address-to-be written on it. But it didn't matter, I thought. I'd go back to the barn and get it when we got ready to leave. And then Sam and I would just walk out nearly to the highway, and there we would wait until Danny came. I wanted to see him once more before we left.

I hadn't heard the slightest noise from anywhere in the house, and I was hesitant about leaving the room. Maybe the woman was still sleeping. I didn't want to disturb her. So far, Sam had been very quiet, probably because I'd given him a cookie. But after a while he began to really wake up, and he dropped the rest of the cookie onto the bed and said, "Sam t'irsty. Sam go pee."

"In a little while," I promised him. But of course that didn't mean a whole lot to Sam.

"Sam go *pee*," he insisted a moment later.

Knowing I had little choice, I picked him up and started for the door. At the same time, I heard that loud click, and the door opened.

The woman stood in the doorway, and for the first time I got a reasonably good look at her.

She was tall and thin with iron-gray hair combed straight back from her face and tied at the back of her neck. She wore a faded cotton print housedress and battered slippers. Her cheekbones jutted from a long, thin face, and her thin-lipped mouth was unusually wide and unsmiling. She wasn't attractive, but I felt that she wasn't as old as she appeared to be. The only really disturbing thing about her appearance was her eyes. They were large and kind of sunken, and they darted this way and that, never really settling anywhere. It gave her a look almost as if she was frightened, or at the least, insecure and nervous.

"Good morning," I said. Sam stared at her, wide-eyed.

She merely nodded. "Is the baby ready for breakfast?" she asked in that odd scratchy voice.

"He needs to go to the bathroom first," I said.

She inclined her head in the direction of the bed. "There's a pot under the bed," she said. "He'll have to use that. You too. Come out when you're finished."

She pushed the door almost closed then, and uncomprehending, I looked under the bed. Sure enough, a kind of bucket stood there. It was white porcelain with a wire handle and a fitted lid. I could hardly believe it; was this what I'd seen references to in old literature, a "chamber pot"? But surely no one used such things anymore! If she had no bathroom inside, there surely must be an old outside toilet somewhere, like the one back at the house where Danny stayed.

Nevertheless, she had said we'd have to use it, so I tried to show Sam that he must sit on the pot. He didn't like it one bit. The thing scooted on the floor, and I suppose the instability scared him. At any rate, he wouldn't "go pee" in the chamber pot, and finally I gave up and put his pants on again.

Tentatively I pushed the door open, noting the closing mechanism as I did so. It was a heavy dead-bolt lock, the kind Uncle Ed had on the doors back home because, as he'd said, "With all the good-for-nothing bums around nowadays, you can't trust nobody not to steal you blind." As if there'd been anything in that house worth stealing! Even the television was nothing but a piece of junk!

Surely she hadn't really locked that door the night before. Of course not; what a silly idea.

She was in the kitchen, cooking an egg in an ancient skillet. When it was done, she put it on a plate and motioned for me to feed it to Sam. I sat, and looked around for bread or milk. There was nothing; the table was bare except for that single plate and a spoon.

I cut the egg up and offered Sam a bite. He seemed uncomfortable, looking this way and that, but he really was hungry, and at last he began to eat. Soon the plate was clean. The woman had stood watching, her arms crossed. When Sam had finished the egg, she turned back to the stove, and in a moment she placed a bowl of oatmeal in front of me.

"For you," she muttered.

I wasn't hungry, and I was also getting very nervous. But I felt that it would be better if I tried to eat, so I lifted a spoonful to my mouth. The woman stood as before, watching me. I wondered if her eyes darted around all the time, or only when someone was looking at her. . . .

It tasted horrid. There was little if any salt in the oatmeal, and not a grain of sugar or any milk. It was a thick and gluey mess, and I had to force myself to swallow it. I managed to eat a few spoonfuls, however, before I simply could not endure any more.

"That was very good," I said. "Thank you for fixing us breakfast."

Again she didn't respond. She took the bowl and spoon, and when she turned, I saw something that sent chills all over me. It wasn't anything really, and I mentally scolded myself for thinking there was anything unusual. It was only a bunch of keys.

She wore a belt, a narrow leather one that did not match her dress, and on this belt a ring of keys hung. I didn't know why the sight of those keys had disturbed me, but they had. The key ring had evidently been the source of the jingling sound I had heard the night before.

I had put Sam down while I ate the oatmeal, but he had stayed right there, hanging on to me. He hadn't said a single word.

"I guess we'd better be going now," I said to the woman. "I really do appreciate your giving us a place to sleep, and the breakfast. And again, I apologize for staying in your barn without permission. But it's time for Sam and me to go home now. So I'll just get my things. Then we'll go."

She nodded, and I got to my feet. Then she said, "Can I hold the baby while you get ready?" As it had been the night before when she had spoken of Sam, her voice had a softer, gentler sound, and I was touched. Odd she might be, but the woman did really seem kind of attracted to Sam.

"Well sure," I said, "but he's a little bashful. He might not be willing to go to you, since you're still a stranger to him." That was a lie of course, about Sam being bashful. But I didn't think he *would* go to her, the way he was staying close to me, and I didn't want to hurt her feelings.

She leaned down and reached one hand out to him, and

with a glance at me, he took her hand. Pleased that he hadn't turned away as I had expected, I said, "It's okay, Sam. She's a nice lady."

Silly, inane words, but he appeared to understand. And when she went on to pick him up, he offered no resistance.

Smiling, I went back into the bedroom where we had slept. I picked up the cookie crumbs, putting them in my pocket for lack of a better place. Then I smoothed the covers and lifted the backpack. Then just as I was settling it comfortably in place, I heard the loud and ominous click once more. Whirling around, I went to the door and pushed, but it wouldn't open. I turned the knob frantically.

Nothing. I was locked in!

Chapter Twelve

FOR THE LONGEST time I simply stood there in front of the door. I was stunned. My brain didn't seem to want to function at all. My hands went to the door knob again; my hands didn't believe the door was really locked. But it would not open, and at last, but sluggishly, it was like all of the parts of me began to get themselves reassembled. The door was *locked*.

Feeling foolish, I rapped on the door with my knuckles. Surely it was accidental, surely the woman hadn't locked me in that bedroom deliberately!

"The door's locked," I called out, wondering whether I sounded as silly and as scared as I felt. "Would you open it please?"

There was no answer.

I knocked louder. "Please open the door!" I called out louder than before. "Sam and I really do have to leave now, so won't you open the door for me please?"

I waited, with an ear pressed against the wood, and finally I heard her voice, unpleasant in tone, but she sounded hesitant, unsure.

"I want you to stay a little bit longer," she said. "You can leave after . . . after a while."

"But we can't," I yelled. "We have to leave right *now*, so you've just got to let me out."

"In a little while," she replied. "I just want to hold the baby a little bit. Then you can go."

I thought I'd been confused a few minutes earlier, but that was nothing compared to the crazy and disconnected thoughts that went flashing through my mind at her peculiar remarks. I was locked in. The house was dark. The woman out there "holding the baby" was surely insane. There was no bathroom. She didn't put sugar or milk in oatmeal. The window was boarded up. Sam was out there with a crazy woman, and I was actually, unbelievably, a prisoner in a goofy little house with a high-pitched roof and with an actual, honest-to-god Edgar Allan Poe *chamber pot* under the bed!

It didn't make a bit of sense, and I felt so mixed up that I wasn't even scared or angry or anything a person might expect to be. I felt empty and stupid and unbelieving. This could not be real! It was a dream, a fairy tale, a bad movie that couldn't decide whether it was more horrifying or hysterical.

Except . . . I wasn't laughing.

I simply *had* to get my mind to working right, and quickly. But the whole thing was just so utterly *stupid*! What was I going to do?

The house was deathly quiet. Had she gone away, or was she still standing on the other side of the door? She'd been wearing house slippers; she could've walked away without making any noise. She must have done that, or I would have heard Sam. He couldn't possibly be quiet for longer than a couple of minutes at a time.

Sam . . .

That's when I began to get scared again. My hands trembled and my knees grew so weak that I had to go and sit on the bed. For a little while I felt smothered, and my heart pounded at a furious rate. Was Sam in danger? Obviously the woman was as nutty as a fruitcake; how could I know whether or not she was actually dangerous? There was no way to tell.

I didn't really think she was, because of her hesitant manner and the way she seemed unsure of herself with Sam but drawn to him at the same time. Still, the woman was . . .

she was *crazy*; that was the word that kept coming back to me.

It seemed like she didn't know much about children, the way she'd kept referring to Sam as "the baby." Well, he was a baby, in a way, but it still sounded odd. And why in heaven's name was there no real light in the house? Why were the windows covered? I'd never even heard of such weird things before, and I didn't have the tiniest idea of how to consider them.

At last the strength began to return to my legs, and I wondered how much time had passed. I had no idea whether it had been ten minutes or an hour. The house was still breathlessly silent, and that very silence began to irritate me and to frighten me at the same time. A part of me wanted to yell and scream for help, but something kept me quiet.

I got up and began to explore the room. My eyes had become accustomed to the near-darkness, yet I still couldn't really see very much. First I went to the window, or rather to the boards that covered what I was sure must have been a window. Maybe I could loosen a board and let some light into the room. I kept thinking that if only I had some light, I could think more clearly.

The boards were wide, and rough to the touch, but they had been neatly sawed at the ends. I could not really see the nailheads, but I could tell by touch that they were big, and my hopes fell. I'd never be able to pull them loose.

I tried anyway, hooking my fingertip over the ends of a board and tugging until I was out of breath. Once I thought I felt it give just a little, but I could not move it any more, and I decided I must've imagined that it had ever moved at all.

I tried the other boards that I could reach, but they were all solidly fixed, and I began to give up. I went back to the bed to sit and think, but my thinking was singularly unproductive, and in a moment I was at the heavy, old-fashioned dresser. It had a huge mirror with a jagged and discolored crack all down one side of it. I looked at my dim reflection, and I thought that the distortion in my face where the cracked glass reflected me was remarkably accurate at the moment. Some perverse part of me almost smiled.

There was not one single item on top of the dresser, and I expected to find the drawers as empty, but they weren't. On the upper level there were two short, deep drawers side by side. The first one contained odds and ends of clothing. I found several pairs of ladies' gloves. Most were ordinary cloth or leather gloves, and some looked new while others had been worn. I found underwear there, too, and nylon stockings. They weren't pantyhose, but regular stockings. Rummaging through all this quickly, I found at the bottom of the drawer yet another pair of gloves, but these were different. They were probably a faded white. I couldn't tell for sure, but I could see and feel that they were of the most delicate lace I had ever touched, and I wondered: Were these a memento of some terribly important occasion in the woman's life? A wedding, perhaps?

But it didn't matter, and I closed the drawer and opened the one next to it. What was I looking for? I didn't know. Anything—anything at all that might tell me something about the owner of the things I pawed through, or suggest some action that I might take.

The second drawer was more interesting than the first. It contained neatly stacked photographs, many of them in old frames, and bundles of what appeared to be letters. I looked at the pictures. There were several really old black and white prints of people standing still and formal for the photographer. There were men, women, and children, and I thought they were probably pictures of long-dead relatives. I wished for light to see them better, but there was none. I stacked the pictures on top of the dresser as I looked at them. At the bottom I found more recent pictures, though they were far from new. These appeared to be snapshots rather than the rigid, formally posed older photographs.

There must have been at least twenty pictures of a little kid, a boy I thought. These were not in frames. They seemed to all be pictures of the same child, covering a couple of years or so of his life. I put them on the dresser top. The last two pictures were of a young couple. The man wore a military uniform of some kind, and the woman, tall and looking up at the even taller man in both snapshots, couldn't be anyone else but the crazy woman who had locked me in and who was somewhere on the other side of the door, with Sam. In the pictures she was much younger, but I could see the thin face with the prominent cheekbones and the wide mouth well enough to know it had to be her.

The two long drawers below were filled with tightly packed white sheets, towels, and lots of curtains. I didn't pay much attention to those things. I wanted to read the letters or at least to look at them, but it seemed to be too difficult, and besides, they were surely personal, and surely important to her, to have been kept so carefully.

Personal? Important? What did I care? The woman had locked me up, and she might be dangerous to Sam and me both! That should cancel out the rules of good manners for me, too, shouldn't it? Still, I put the letters on the dresser and left them there.

With all my nosing around, I still didn't know anything, and Sam and I were still prisoners. What did she have on my mind, I wondered. She had said that she just wanted to "hold the baby" for a little while, then we could leave. It could be that she'd been telling the truth, and I hoped for that. But in my heart I was terrified, and I couldn't quite make myself believe that it would be that simple.

By the time I had struggled with the boards at the window and searched the dresser drawers, quite a bit of time had gone by, I figured. I sat on the edge of the bed again, tired and trembling. A couple of times I thought I heard something, but when I tensed, listening, all was quiet. I sat for a long time, trying to solve or at least to find some glimmer of understanding of my dilemma, but nothing except the wildest imaginings came to my mind. Then I did hear something.

It was Sam, and he was crying.

I knew he must be in another room somewhere besides the kitchen, for the sound of his crying was muffled. I could tell that he was not crying from pain, and since I could not comfort him, I was grateful. He was fretful, from the sound of it, whimpering more than actually crying, and I thought that it must be nearing noon and he was getting sleepy. Maybe he would drift off to sleep quickly; that would give me an hour or two of feeling that he was probably all right.

How confused he must be feeling, though! I had been right with him almost every moment since the day Mr. Patterson and the lady social worker had first brought him to our house, and although he'd always been warm and trusting with nearly everyone, he was surely feeling lost, and wondering why I had deserted him.

The crying grew louder, the angry, frustrated crying that can go on and on, and suddenly a horrifying image came to mind. I remembered Uncle Ed's harsh words: "I'll give that brat something to cry about. . . ." Would Sam's crying irritate the strange woman? Might she possibly react to Sam's crying as Uncle Ed had done?

Or maybe . . . just possibly, if Sam's crying did bother her . . . maybe she would let us go!

I hurried to the door and pounded on it as hard as I could. "Hey lady!" I called foolishly, not knowing what I ought to call her, "Hey lady! Come here!"

I expected that she either wouldn't hear me or that, hearing, she might not respond, but in a moment I could almost feel that she was near. Then she spoke.

"What do you want?" she asked. She sounded grouchy.

"Haven't you had enough time with Sam?" I asked. "You said you only wanted to hold him for a little while and then we could go. It's been long enough, hasn't it?"

For a long time she didn't answer me at all. When she did, it wasn't much help.

"Wait a little bit longer," she said. "Then you can go. Just a little while longer."

"But I can hear Sam crying," I said. "If you don't want us to leave, we can stay for a while. But unlock the door, please. Let me out so I can take care of Sam."

"In a little while, I said," she repeated in that same tone.

"The baby is all right. Don't worry about the baby. I'm taking good care of him."

"But he's not used to you yet," I tried to reason. "Sam's used to having me take care of him, don't you see? He's crying because he's wondering where I am."

"He'll be quiet in a minute," she said.

"Lady, this doesn't make any sense," I said then, and I was getting awfully frantic and trying to keep it out of my voice. I was trying to sound normal and reasonable. "It's not good for kids . . . for babies to be frightened, and Sam must be feeling pretty scared, don't you think? Surely you don't really want to make him feel so unhappy, do you?"

"He'll be quiet in a minute," she repeated.

There was no reasoning with the woman! She sounded like a broken record with her repeated promises of "in a little while," and "in a minute," and I couldn't stand it any more. Anger flooded through me in a shocking and uncontrollable wave, and I pounded the door with my clenched hands, screaming, "Let me *out* of here, you crazy old witch! Let me out of here right now!" Over and over I screamed and pounded, until my voice grew hoarse and I became aware of the pain in both my hands. I slipped to the floor, leaning against that awful locked door, sobbing with helplessness.

My hands were red and raw as though they'd been sanded, and the skin was tender and painful. My throat hurt something awful, and I had to swallow over and over to keep from vomiting. I was so angry, so scared, so *confused*.

When there wasn't a single tear left in my body, I continued sitting there. What else was there to do? Nothing! I couldn't do one single thing for Sam or for myself. I stared toward that boarded window, wishing again for light. A person could go as crazy as the woman was, living in this half darkness all the time. If only I had some light!

Then I noticed something that I didn't recognize immediately. It appeared that there was a spot of light just hanging there in the air in the middle of the room. I could see dust motes floating there. But where was the little spot of light coming from?

I finally figured it out. Evidently there was a crack between a couple of the boards over the window. If there was a crack, it was between two boards that were higher than my head, but I felt absolutely desperate for light . . . even a little speck of light.

Scrambling to my feet, I went to the window, wondering how I could get high enough to find the actual crack. I climbed onto the bed, and sure enough, I could see it. A crack about four inches long, maybe a quarter-inch wide. But I was too far away to actually look out through the crack.

I tried moving the bed, but it was too heavy and I was in too much of a hurry to take the mattress and stuff off so I could move it. Then I thought of the dresser drawers.

They too were heavy, but I managed to get them out of the dresser and stacked on top of one another. I climbed up and put my face to the crack between the boards. Mercifully, there was no newspaper over the window behind the boards, and at last I could see light . . . real, honest, clear, bright, beautiful light!

I enjoyed just having found the tiny source of light so much that it took a minute for me to think of what I could actually see from the crack, and when I looked, I was pleased to at least see something I'd seen before. The barn. The weeds were high between the house and the barn, but I was looking from a little extra height, and I could see the door, and . . . and the person coming through it.

It was Danny. Dejectedly he left the barn. He paused once, looking toward the house, and that's when I began to yell.

"Danny!" I screamed, over and over. "Danny! Help! Danny!"

"Stop that yelling! Stop that yelling right now, if you want me to *ever* let you go," the woman's voice came through the door, harsh and threatening.

I stopped, but not because of what she'd said. Danny hadn't heard me. He had just stood looking toward the house for a little bit while I yelled for him. Then he had turned away, his shoulders slumped, and started up the road. Then I couldn't see him anymore.

Chapter Thirteen

MORE TIME PASSED and I stayed quiet. I was too dispirited to make any more fuss. To think that Danny had been there, only a few yards away from Sam and me, and I hadn't been able to make him hear me! In all the frantic confusion of the morning, I had forgotten that he would be coming. Not that it mattered; there had been no way for me to get his attention anyway.

But I *had* left him a kind of message, and when I thought of it, his address on the scrap of paper I'd been holding when I went to sleep in the barn, my heart lifted. Of course I knew it was possible that he hadn't found the paper, but it would have been lying in plain sight where I had surely dropped it. He should have seen it easily . . . if it hadn't gotten covered in the hay the night before when the crazy woman had come and woke us up. And when he saw that I had left his address-to-be behind, he would know that something had to be wrong, wouldn't he?

Unless . . . oh no! I hoped that he *hadn't* found it after all, because he might get the idea that I had left it behind on purpose, and if he thought that, I couldn't bear to imagine how it might be. He'd told me how important it was for me to write to him, and he'd said it had been my reaction to his stealing that caused him to stop. Now, if he concluded that I had left his address on purpose, that I didn't really care what became of him . . . the possibilities were too awful to consider. Either way, there didn't seem to be much for me to look forward to. It was almost a certainty that I had made things even worse by yelling at Danny. Knowing he'd been out there at the barn, the woman would probably be more suspicious and defensive than before.

The minutes dragged by, and I lay across the bed staring at the spot of light hanging in the air and trying without any success not to think at all. So far, my thinking had gotten me nowhere; I'd only been going around in mental circles. As Danny had said just the day before, I'd been like a cat chasing its tail.

At some point I must have fallen into a dazed nothingness, and when the voice came from the other side of the door, it took a moment for her question to penetrate my foggy brain.

"What's your name, girl?" the woman was asking.

"It's Marylou," I finally replied, sitting up.

"Are you all right now?"

I was puzzled. What did she mean? Of course I was all right, if being shut up in a house with a person like her could be considered "all right."

"I said are you all right now? Are you going to start screaming again? There's nobody out there, you know. There's never anybody except the grocery boy, and he isn't due for another week. So there's no use in your yelling. If you won't yell anymore, I'll let you have something to eat."

Eat? I hadn't thought of food, but when she mentioned it, I realized that my stomach felt awfully hollow. Then it suddenly occurred to me that she must not have realized that Danny *had* been there. She thought that I'd been yelling in some general hope of attracting attention, and that realization cheered me up.

"I won't yell anymore. I promise," I said, practically holding my breath in hopes that she would believe me.

I heard the click of the lock a moment later, and I stood, fearfully waiting to see what would happen. The door swung open, but she stood there with a hand still on the doorknob.

"It's not time for you to leave with the baby yet," she said, "but if you'll be good, I'll let you come out for a while."

"I'll be good," I said. Behind my back, my fingers were crossed. I would be "good" at least until I had a chance to get away.

She nodded, indicating that I should come into the kitchen. It was all I could do not to run. I wanted to see Sam, but I didn't want to antagonize the woman, at least not until I understood her a little better.

The kitchen was empty, and the woman pointed to yet another door leading into another room. It was closed but not locked, although I noticed that it too had a dead bolt on it. I pushed the door open, and that room, too, a living room, was almost dark, but I saw Sam. He was sitting in the floor surrounded by makeshift toys. But he wasn't playing; he was just sitting there.

He looked up and saw me, and he came to life, scrambling up and shouting, "Ma'Lou! Ma'Lou!" as if we'd been separated for a year instead of the biggest part of a day. I leaned down and he practically leapt into my arms, hugging me so tight I could hardly breathe. My eyes stung with tears. I had been so afraid of . . . I didn't know *what* I'd been afraid of, but the relief at seeing for myself that he wasn't harmed was really something.

"I told you I would take care of the baby," the woman said from behind me. She sounded proud, almost triumphant.

I didn't know what to say. It was as if she didn't realize what she had actually done. She thought everything was fine! It was idiotic, but I felt that I should play along, not letting her see how I really felt.

"I did take care of the baby," she said again.

"Yes. Yes, of course you did," I said, feeling my way with her. "Sam is just fine. You've taken good care of him."

"You stay in here," she said then. "I'll fix us some supper." Then she went back into the kitchen, closing the door behind her.

I looked around. We were in the side of the house that I had been looking at the day before when I had started toward the house to explore, then changed my mind. The furniture

93

was like that of the bedroom, heavy and old-fashioned, and the floor was covered with handmade rugs, the kind Aunt Bonnie had called ''rag rugs.'' It was awfully dark in there, and I found a light switch near the front door and turned it on, but my hopes were useless. This room too had only a tiny light bulb. It barely helped at all.

The front door—the one leading onto the littered porch, was locked of course, but it was a different sort of lock that could be opened from the inside only with a key. The key would be on the ring hanging from the woman's belt.

I examined the windows next. There were two, and they were covered with heavy dark brown drapes. I pulled the drapes aside, and wonder of wonders, there was a little bit of light! I could not see out because of the newspaper plastered over the glass, but a bit of illumination came through. When I realized that it must be late afternoon or evening, I knew that even that bit of light would be gone soon. I tucked one panel of the drapes behind a chair, to keep the light as long as I could.

All this time Sam kept patting my cheeks with his chubby little hands, then hugging me tight again. He was happy, and I didn't want him to feel my fear.

There was no television, no radio, no telephone. A long sofa took up one whole wall, and there were three big chairs and a couple of tables in the room. One table near the door held a stack of mail. I picked up an envelope and took it to the window. It was addressed to Mrs. Jane Abington. The return address listed the Swifton State Bank. The letter had not been opened. At the table again I saw other unopened mail, all addressed to Jane Abington. Several letters were from the bank. I noticed three others from a doctor's office in Swifton. I wondered how she got her mail and why she hadn't opened it.

The door from the kitchen opened then, and the woman came into the room. Immediately she went to the window and put the drape back in place. By then it made little difference.

''You can come and eat now,'' she said.

I followed her into the kitchen. She had fried some bacon and fixed canned beans and stewed potatoes. There wasn't much of any of it, but at least she had set three plates, and we all sat down. Sam insisted on staying on my lap.

She began eating, not looking at us until Sam said, "Eat, Ma'Lou! Sam eat. Sam *'ungry*!" At that her head came up and for once her eyes remained focused—on Sam.

"He can talk," she said. She was obviously surprised. Maybe she hadn't understood when he called my name earlier, but had he said nothing else all day long? Amazing!

"Yes, he can talk," I said. Then remembering Danny's pleasure when Sam had spoken his name, I said, "Sam, can you say 'Jane Abington'?"

"D'ane Abington," he mimicked, and the woman laughed out loud! It was the strangest sound. I suddenly felt sure that Mrs. Jane Abington had not laughed in a very long time, and I was glad that Sam had been so cooperative.

The food was all right; it was awfully bland, but I was hungry. Sam ate with enthusiasm, too, but Mrs. Abington didn't eat a dozen bites. When we were finished, she began cleaning the table. I was able to put Sam down to play at last, and I began helping her. I thought she was surprised, but she didn't speak until we were finished washing the few dishes. The kitchen was equipped with a double sink, but there was no running water. She poured water sparingly from a big metal bucket.

"Why don't you have running water?" I asked her, because the silence was becoming unbearable.

She cleared her throat. "They put stuff in it. Chemicals," she muttered. "There's a pump outside. Good water there."

So she was afraid of the county water system, and she got her own water from the pump outside. The bucket was nearly empty, and I wondered when she would go out to get more, and whether I might be able to get away then. It wasn't long before I found out.

A clock sat on the top of the refrigerator, and she took it down, bringing it close to her face. Even in the near darkness

I could see the big numbers on the clock from where I stood. She really could not see well at all.

"It's dark now," she muttered. "Time to get some water." I didn't reply, and she stood there, apparently thinking it over. Then she poured the remaining water into a bowl and handed me the bucket.

"You get the water," she said. "The pump's that direction." She pointed.

I nodded. "I saw it yesterday," I said. "Will one bucketful be enough? How do you wash your clothes?"

Again she thought it over. "The baby's clothes need washing?" she asked.

"Yes," I said. "Mine, too. If there's a laundromat not too far away, I'll be glad to . . ."

"Can't do that," she said quickly. "We'll wash them here, in the sink. That's how I do it. You get some water."

I tried to keep the excitement from my voice. "Sure," I said. Then I leaned down to pick Sam up. "C'mere Sam," I said. "Let's go get some water."

Suddenly she was between us. "He'll stay in here with me," she said.

Reluctantly I decided not to argue. If I was "good," maybe she would relax and begin trusting me. I was afraid to try to insist. She might manage to lock me in again.

"All right," I said. "That's probably better anyway. The night air might not be good for Sam." I felt stupid saying such things, but it seemed to work. She went to the door and unlocked it. Again I was disappointed. I had hoped she might take the key ring off her belt, and I could possibly get it away from her, but it was on one of those chains that pull out, and she didn't have to take it off.

I heard Sam protesting when I left the house, but I would be right back, so I didn't worry. It was awfully dark outside, but the fresh air felt good, and I finally made my way in the darkness to the pump. I had never used such a pump before, but I had seen them in movies, so I set the bucket under the spout and began to work the handle. In a moment the water gushed out and soon the bucket was full. It was heavy, but I managed to lift it and carry it back to the house. Mrs. Abington had been waiting at the door for me. I heard the click of the lock just before it opened. This woman had an obsession with locks! She had locked the door behind me. It was hard to believe, and it made me increasingly nervous.

Inside, I poured the water into the two sinks, and waited for what I was to do next. "Get more," she said. "We'll have to have enough for tomorrow."

On the second trip for water, I was more puzzled than before. She had said we would need water enough for tomorrow. Why? Why couldn't she go out and fill the bucket any time she happened to run out of water? Like everything else that was happening, there was no sense to it. I had to try to understand, I thought, but the puzzle was becoming more complicated all the time!

Chapter Fourteen

WHEN I RETURNED with the second bucketful of water, I found that Mrs. Abington had another chore for me to do. She told me to get Sam's and my clothes. They were in the bedroom, and I was afraid to go in there; maybe it was a trick and she would hurry to lock the door behind me. When I hesitated, though, she said, "Go on, get your clothes. I can't wash them until I have them!"

I could see no evidence or even a suggestion that she meant to lock me in, although I didn't even begin to trust her. How can you trust someone who behaves in such unpredictable and illogical ways? Still, I went into the bedroom and emptied the backpack, quickly grabbing all our dirty clothes. When I returned with them to the kitchen, she took them from me and put some into the sinkful of water. Then she turned back to face me.

"I'll do this," she said, indicating the laundry. "You go and get the pots from my bedroom and yours."

"The pots?" I asked, not understanding.

"From under the beds," she said. "Empty them in the toilet outside, then wash them at the pump."

Gross! She meant that I was to empty and then wash the chamber pots, and I couldn't imagine a more distasteful task.

"If you have a bath . . . a toilet outside, why don't you just use it?" I asked. "It would be so much simpler and . . . and cleaner."

"Because the toilet's outside," she said, shaking her head in impatience at my ignorance.

She had answered my question, but it was no answer. Evidently she thought it was. "Well, go on," she said. "It's dark now, so get on with it!" Then before I could even think of any alternative, she lifted Sam and stood waiting for me to go.

I went into the living room and turned to what I assumed was the door to her room. But the door wouldn't open.

"The door's locked," I called out.

In a moment she was there with her keys. "Don't yell," she said as she fumbled to insert the key into the lock on her door. "I don't like noise; it gives me a headache." She had a difficult time with the lock because she was still holding Sam, who wiggled with impatience, and of course she couldn't see what she was doing either.

"Here, let me help you," I offered, stepping close to her.

"Get away!" she barked. I moved back, startled. I really had only meant to help.

"I'm sorry," I murmured. "I didn't mean any harm."

She turned to glare at me, and this time her eyes didn't turn this way and that. I expected a tirade, but after a moment she turned back to the door and finally got it opened.

"Don't mess with anything," she ordered. "Just get the pot, and hurry up about it."

I did so, only giving the room a quick glance. It was much too dark to see what the room was like anyway, because I hadn't turned the light on.

When I left the house, it was even darker outside, and I did not like going into that old toilet. I thought of spiders and such, and I shivered. Then I almost laughed. I was in this crazy situation with this weird woman, and I was worrying about spiders? Lord, I was getting as goofy as she was!

My task was easy enough, but it wasn't pleasant, and I figured that was why she had told me to do it. It would have made more sense to have gotten it done before dark. I wished for sunshine; it seemed to me as if it'd been dark for days and days. What must it be like for Mrs. Abington! The poor woman, so illogical . . . then it hit me: Maybe she was crazy, but not necessarily illogical after all. Logic suggests at least a pattern of behavior, and come to think of it, maybe there was a pattern of sorts. First, she had all the windows covered over and the doors remained closed. Second, the light bulbs in the house were so small as to be practically useless, and there was only one in each room. Third, she had said twice that things that had to be done outside must be done after dark. And finally, she had come to the barn to chase me away in the blackness of the night. It didn't make any *sense* to me, but sensible or not, Mrs. Abington obviously preferred darkness to light. What did it mean, I wondered. Like her obsession with locked doors and her distrust of the county water system, I had never heard of such ridiculous behavior, and I did not know what to make of it except that it was . . . insane?

Sam and I had been there a little less than twenty-four hours, and so far, nothing really horrible had happened to us. But Mrs. Abington evidently meant to keep us there. For how long? And *why* did she want us there? Should I continue trying to go along with her craziness, or would it be smarter for me to put my attention to developing a serious plan of escape?

I could not decide. Everything seemed to depend on what Mrs. Abington really wanted with us and whether or not she was actually dangerous. It was already clear that if I didn't do as she wished, she would use Sam to compel me. She was bright enough to realize that my main concern was Sam, and that I would do anything to keep him safe.

Though being near her was not at all comfortable, I did not actually fear the woman, not at the moment anyway. Yet neither did I feel that either Sam or I was safe.

With my thoughts going in circles, I washed those awful pots at the pump, and when I had finished, I started back toward the house. The closer I came to the door, the more my feet seemed to try to hold me back. I did not want to go back in there. Yet Sam was there, Mrs. Abington's insurance that I would not try to run away.

She had said that nobody ever came there except for the grocery boy, who wasn't due for a while. Still, it was always possible that someone *would* come . . . Danny, for instance. If only I had some way to leave a message, something to say that Sam and I were being held there in the little house, some kind of signal for help! If I had anything, anything at all . . . I felt my pockets and found nothing there except for the crumbled cookie I had stuffed in my jeans pocket that morning. Disgusted, I dug out the crumbs and threw them onto the ground. They were certainly no signal; mice or birds would soon see to that.

Yet it did give me an idea. Since Mrs. Abington apparently did not want to go outside, perhaps she would send me out again. And if she did, I would take something out with me and leave it as a sign. Maybe . . . just possibly, someone would come.

"What took you so long?" she demanded as soon as I went through the doorway.

"It's too dark to see," I said. "I wanted to do a good job, so I washed them over and over to make sure."

She only grunted in reply, locked the door behind me, and returned to the sink to go on with scrubbing our things.

With her back turned to me and Sam rattling a bunch of jar lids she had laced on a string for him to play with, I looked around quickly. Soon I found what I wanted, a stubby pencil and a pad of paper lying on a shelf. I would write some kind of a note. Then, anxious that she might turn and see what I was up to, I could not think what to write. If I wrote something like, "Help. Sam and I are prisoners," it would be too obvious if she should somehow see it. Yet I had to write something, and the only thing that came to mind was Danny's address, which I had memorized. Quickly I scribbled it on the paper, and signed my name, Marylou Britten. Then I stuffed it into my pocket. Maybe she would let us go, and I wouldn't need it. But then, maybe she wouldn't. . . .

There seemed nothing to do but to wait for whatever she might do or say, so I pulled out a chair and sat down.

It occurred to me that Sam's and my clothes probably

wouldn't be very clean, what with the absence of light and the woman's near-blindness, and for lack of anything better to do, I watched her. She dunked a shirt of mine into the water, sloshed it around a little bit, then wrung it out. Her hands and wrists seemed awfully strong. I wondered that the shirt didn't rip, the way she twisted it with such force.

Then she began to wash Sam's shirt. She handled it differently, sloshing it repeatedly in the water, then scrubbed every inch between her knuckles. At long last she wrung it gently, placing it in the other sink for rinsing. Something about her actions sent chills through me. I had to force myself to speak; my throat seemed unaccustomed to producing a voice.

"Will you be needing more water?" I asked.

She didn't turn around. "Not tonight," she said. "We'll make do with what we have. You can get more tomorrow night." She went on with the washing, unaware that I shivered with sick foreboding. Had I been able to speak, I would surely have said foolish things. Fortunately, my voice had frozen or something. My knees trembled.

She had no intention of letting us leave, although she seemed unaware that she had just told me that. Tomorrow night . . . it seemed a very long time. Anything could happen in another twenty-four hours.

Chapter Fifteen

THE EVENING PASSED mostly in silence except for Sam's occasional chatter and the noise he made while he played. Mrs. Abington had evidently spent the hours while I was locked in the bedroom entirely on entertaining Sam. She had improvised toys for him. A big round box that had once held breakfast oatmeal had become a drum. Several small boxes were connected end-to-end with string, making a kind of train in which he could haul a mixed collection of buttons and other odds and ends, and a big metal mixing spoon was a trailer, pulled behind a "truck" made from a little wooden box.

Either she was more imaginative than she appeared to be, or at some time she'd had some experience with children. I commented on the toys she had made, asking whether she had had any children of her own. She glared at me.

Although she spoke little, her expression did show some animation when she watched Sam. Oddly, silent and unresponsive as she was, Sam appeared to feel comfortable with her.

Mrs. Abington had completed the laundry, hanging our few articles of clothing on a line stretched across the kitchen. Afterward she had insisted that we sit in the living room. "Sit" was the word, for there was nothing more to do. She seemed content to watch Sam as he played, and she made no protest when he was noisy—no mention at all that noise gave her a headache. It was so tiring, so dull, that I began to wish for something to happen—almost anything to occupy my mind.

It began as Sam grew fussy, no longer enjoying the toys or our attention. I knew he was sleepy. Soon he would settle down, and after a couple of minutes of stillness he would fall asleep. I picked him up and held him, patting his back in the gentle rhythm that had always quieted and calmed him, and he began to relax against my chest. My attention was directed completely toward my little Sam, and holding him close gave me as much comfort as it gave him. For a little while I forgot Mrs. Abington, and when Sam finally closed his eyes in sleep, I continued holding him. My thoughts had returned to her by then. I didn't want to admit that Sam was sleeping, for then it would be necessary to learn what was in her mind about how we would spend the night.

Finally I looked her way. I wished that I hadn't for her expression was frozen in hatred.

I was startled. What could be wrong? I didn't dare to ask, and I looked at Sam sleeping so peacefully against me. Someone had to say something to interrupt the bad feelings that seemed to color the air between me and this woman. It would be up to me.

"He's asleep," I finally said. "Isn't he sweet?"

"He can't be your child," she growled in reply. "He *isn't* your child. I know he isn't."

Somehow I knew that it would be a mistake to admit to her that Sam wasn't really mine. It seemed urgent at that moment that she should believe he was my own son, so I lied.

"Of course he's mine," I said lightly, attempting a kind of laugh. "Whatever makes you think he isn't?"

She shrugged, looking away. Then she turned back to face me. "You're too young," she said. "You're not old enough to be a mother. He reminds me of Jas . . ."

"He reminds you of whom?" I prompted her when she didn't continue.

"Never mind," she grunted. "Carry him in to my bed now. He can't be comfortable the way you're holding him."

"Sam sleeps with me," I replied. "I'll take him to the other room." I tried to say it calmly.

She didn't reply, but the bad look came back. I wasn't at all anxious to return to "my bedroom," because I was certain that she would lock the door. But I had to get away from her, so I got to my feet with Sam still in my arms.

"We'll say goodnight now, Mrs. Abington," I said. "I hope you sleep well." As I expected, she made no reply. She didn't even move.

I had put Sam on the bed and crawled in beside him, fully dressed, pulling the sheet over us both, when I heard the lock click. I heard no other sound, not a footstep or a creaking floorboard, and I lay breathless, afraid to move for a very long time. At long last I heard muted sounds from the adjoining room, what I thought might be the clink of the chamber-pot lid, and maybe the creak of bedsprings as she settled down. Still I waited silently until I was sure an hour must have passed without a single sound.

I crept from the bed, and in the darkness I found some cloth that I stuffed in the crack at the bottom of the door. Then I turned the tiny light on and waited to see whether she might respond. Again I heard nothing.

Finally I went to the dresser and found the bundle of letters. I had made up my mind to read them. I needed something, anything to help me, any idea of who or what this woman might really be. There were six envelopes. Some of the letters must really be thick, long ones, I thought.

They weren't letters, at least not what I had expected. The first envelope contained what appeared to be legal documents of some sort. It was difficult to read the fine print, and even when I managed to read it, I didn't fully comprehend. Yet the glimmer of understanding that came through frightened me. There were documents from different courts. One said "summons" at the top. I read references to "the deceased, Mr. James. L. Abington and Master Jason Littlefield Abington," and I grew cold all over when I read that last name. Jason. Had she been about to say that name earlier when she'd said that Sam reminded her of "Jas . . ."? And didn't "Master" mean a young boy? I didn't know why the complicated language and all the rest frightened me so much, but it surely did.

I stuffed the contents back into the envelope and opened the second. More of the same. I didn't even try to read them, but laid them aside and looked into the third envelope.

These too were documents, but they were readable. They were newspaper clippings, old but still clear except for lines where the clippings had been folded. The first one bore a garish headline: WIFE AND MOTHER SUSPECTED IN BRUTAL DOUBLE MURDER.

My stomach churned, and the hair on my arms prickled when I recognized the woman in the accompanying photograph. I almost dropped the papers onto the floor. But I had to know what was there.

I stood in the center of the room, directly under the light, reading all the clippings. Then I looked into the other envelopes and found that they too held newspaper clippings. They were similar. Each envelope contained a set of articles from a single newspaper. Four newspapers had followed the story and reported on every detail, from the tragedy, through investigations, arrest, trial, appeals, and a second trial. Summarized, it was a chillingly horrifying story.

Nine years before, Mrs. Jane Abington, a registered nurse (peculiar and unfriendly, standoffish but a skilled nurse, according to her coworkers at Swifton General Hospital) had returned from grocery shopping to discover the mutilated bodies of her husband James L., and her three-year-old son Jason Littlefield Abington in the backyard of their rural home just outside the Swifton city limits. Mrs. Abington had been treated for shock. Then after a lengthy investigation, she had been arrested for the horrible murders. Nobody recalled having seen her grocery shopping, and someone recalled that she had been very angry and depressed because her husband had been running around with another woman. . . .

She had been convicted, apparently having little defense and unable or unwilling to cooperate in her defense attorney's efforts. She had been sentenced to life in prison and had spent several months in the state penitentiary. Her lawyer had finally gotten a new trial at which Mrs. Abington had been acquitted because of some technicalities involving manipulation or misuse of evidence. The acquittal did not prove her innocence, and with her release from prison, the stories all came to an end, except for one. There was a last article dealing with the fact, clearly resented by the writer, that Mrs. Abington had been able to collect on the two life insurance policies.

I was terrified, and physically sick. So frightened I could hardly think at all, I crept back into bed, drawing Sam close to me. Still I shivered as if freezing, for a very long time. Although I'd been alternately frightened, nervous, and angry at her, I realized as I lay there trembling in fear, that I had not *truly* thought Mrs. Abington was dangerous, but only weird. Now it seemed pretty clear that I'd been wrong. Sam and I had to get away. We had to get away, even if it meant that I would have to . . . to hurt her in some way.

The thought of such a possibility was sickening to me, even in that desperate situation. I had left home because of physical violence, the thoughtless, cruel infliction of pain. Now I had to contemplate the possibility myself, to even try to plan how I might be able to do it.

I fell asleep at last, then awoke very early, long before Sam stirred. The whole horrid story in all its gruesome detail came back to me the instant I awoke. Again terror swept over me. Yet somehow I had to control it. I simply *had* to keep her from knowing what I had learned!

I slipped from the bed and replaced all the letters and the stack of photographs as well. I looked closely at the pictures of the little boy. He was slender and blond. He did not even remotely resemble Sam. Yet on the backs of some of the pictures, his name was written: Jason Littlefield Abington.

When she came at last to unlock the door, I could hardly bear to look at her. All I could think of was the way she glared, the severity of her thin-lipped mouth, and the harshness of her voice. But I tried to act normal. She paid little attention to me. She was only interested in Sam.

Again she prepared an egg for him, but she insisted on feeding him instead of allowing me to do it. She didn't fix any of the oatmeal for me as she had done on the preceeding day.

"There's no more oatmeal, and only a few eggs," she said abruptly. "You'll have to do without until lunchtime." At first I thought perhaps she intended to starve me, then I realized that she didn't eat anything either.

I looked everywhere for possible weapons. When I offered to wash the few utensils she had used in the kitchen so I could find a . . . sharp knife . . . she told me to leave them alone. I didn't argue. By then I had seen a hammer on a shelf. The thought of even touching the thing, knowing what I might have to do with it, was upsetting. But I would. If I had to do it, I would. . . .

The day passed in misery and anxiety. Once she asked why I was so "jumpy" and I said that I was anxious to go home. I watched her carefully. There was no reaction. "If I don't get home today or tonight, my family will have the police looking for me," I ventured cautiously.

"Police don't know anything," she growled. Nothing else.

Darkness came at last. She announced it after looking at the clock again. We still hadn't used all the water, and I was afraid she would not want me to go out. But of course there were the pots to be emptied and washed. This time I was eager to do it.

Again she held Sam while she unlocked the door, giving me no opportunity to take him out with me. I hurried out into the darkness, and fresh, clean air had never felt so good. I emptied the pots, then quickly went to the side of the old toilet. I had found a thumbtack stuck in the bedroom wall, and had carried it in my pocket most of the day. I used it to attach the paper with my name and Danny's address on it, to the outside wall of the toilet, desperately wishing there was something else I could do.

I washed the pots at the pump as I had done the night before, and I deliberately banged the lids, knowing all the while that my efforts would be pointless. Then I returned to the house. It was quite awhile before she came to let me in.

"I could have left you out there," she said when I was inside, "and I will if you make any more noise."

"I only dropped it," I said. "It's so dark . . . I didn't mean to do it."

"You did it on purpose," she replied. "You think somebody will come, but they won't. Nobody comes here. I told you that. People don't like me. They're afraid. But don't worry. I'm going to let you go. Before noon tomorrow, you'll be gone."

Chapter Sixteen

"BEFORE NOON TOMORROW, you'll be gone." If I hadn't read those newspaper clippings, what she had said would have sounded reassuring, but now those words inspired nothing but more fear. She could have meant practically anything, and I felt sure that she hadn't meant what I'd been hoping for.

We spent the evening like the preceding one, sitting in the living room watching Sam. But this time I wasn't bored. My mind was busy enough, for I had devised a plan, or at least the beginning of a plan. I would have to be very careful though, and Mrs. Abington would have to cooperate by letting me keep Sam with me to sleep. Perhaps she would do what I wanted her to do if I could avoid making her angry.

The time passed too slowly, and I was both anxious and fearful about the arrival of bedtime. Again the woman seemed to be content just watching Sam, but when he grew fussy, she picked him up immediately. I had been afraid of that, and afraid it would lead to her insisting that Sam sleep in her bed.

Sam, however, wasn't at all cooperative. He did not want to sleep yet, or perhaps he wanted me to hold him. He wouldn't sit still, and finally she let him get back onto the floor. I noticed the stack of unopened mail on the table, and to distract her attention from Sam, I mentioned it.

"You haven't opened your mail," I said. "If your eyes

bother you too badly . . . would you like me to read it to you?"

She didn't reply for a moment. Had I angered her? But no, when she finally spoke, her voice was nearly soft. It appeared that she was touched by my offer.

"The grocery boy brings it out twice a month," she said. "I broke my glasses awhile back. That's why I can't see to read, but I never get any real mail anyway. You might . . . you might just tell me who the letters are from, though."

I went to get the stack of letters, and just as I moved to stand beneath the light, I heard a brief clatter of noise from out back. She looked up, startled.

"Did you hear that?" she asked. "Somebody's out there!" She was obviously frightened, and for some reason that surprised me.

"If you like, I'll look outside," I said.

She hesitated, then nodded, getting to her feet. "Don't *go* out," she muttered. "Just look."

I followed her to the kitchen, and when she unlocked the door, I leaned out to look. I saw nothing, and I was disappointed. I had hoped someone *was* out there.

"There's nobody," I said. "It was probably just a stray dog or cat or something."

She locked the door again and we returned to the living room, but she seemed nervous. Her eyes darted around even worse than usual, so I picked up the mail again. I didn't want her to be agitated, so I began reading the return addresses to her.

"There are several letters from the bank," I said. "Should I open them?"

"No," she replied. "I know what they are. Just statements about interest and that kind of thing."

"How about these from the insurance, or the three from the doctor?" I asked. "They might be important."

She cleared her throat. "They don't matter either," she said. "The doctor wants me to take his medicine. That's all those letters are. But I don't need it. The medicine makes me . . . sleepy."

111

"But if the doctor thinks you need medicine . . ."

"I know as much about it as he does," she muttered, and I thought maybe she was right. After all, she'd been a registered nurse, according to those clippings. . . .

Sam got up from the floor and came to wrap his arms around my legs. "Sam go pee," he said.

That was better than I'd hoped for, if she would trust me to take him without following us as she sometimes did. "I'll just take him in the bedroom," I said, taking his hand.

She didn't reply or get up, and we went into the kitchen. Quickly I took the hammer from the shelf, then we went on to the bedroom. I slid the pot out from under the bed, and Sam grabbed the lid off. He had finally gotten used to sitting on it, and while he tugged his training pants down, I slipped the hammer beneath the mattress on our bed.

When he was finished, he tried to climb onto the bed, and I helped him. Wonder of wonders, he crawled to the other side and snuggled onto the pillow. I sat beside him, gently rubbing his back, and in a moment I could tell by the even rhythm of his breathing that he was nearly asleep.

Then Mrs. Abington appeared in the doorway and stood watching. I put a finger to my lips, and she nodded and turned away. She did not lock the door. She didn't even close it.

I wondered what that could mean. Again, if I hadn't read the clippings, it would have seemed like a good thing. As it was though, knowing what I knew about her, I was more afraid than ever. With the door unlocked, she could come into the room during the night without waking us; she moved about so silently. . . .

I would not give her the chance. Sleepy as I was from the restless night before, I intended to remain awake.

It seemed an awfully long time before I heard the faint sounds from her room indicating that she had gone to bed. Then again I had to wait and wait until I thought she would simply have to be asleep.

At last I decided it was time, but I had no confidence. It was a "now or never" kind of choice. I slipped from the bed

112

and closed the door silently, then turned on the light and got the hammer from beneath the mattress.

At the window I hooked the claws of the hammer under the end of one of the boards, and pulled hard and steadily. There was very little sound, and at first I couldn't believe it, but at last I knew it was true: the nail was coming out! When it was loosened and nearly all the way out, I paused to listen. I had thought I'd heard something, but apparently it had been my fearful imagination.

I hooked the hammer at the other end of the board and began tugging at it. That one was harder, and when the nail finally began to give, it made a screeching sound. I stopped, breathless, waiting for any other sound. After a long time of silence, I began again. This time there was no noise, and I pulled the nail all the way out. Soon the board was completely off the window, and I laid it carefully on the floor.

Excited by my success, I stooped to look out. I couldn't see much, but I could *see*. The space was only a foot wide, though. I would have to remove at least one more board. Then maybe I'd be able to simply open the window and climb through it with Sam.

I was sure I'd seen no screens from the outside of the house. If I *could* open the window by removing just one more of the boards, it wouldn't be impossible to slip away from this crazy little house and its crazier owner. As an absolutely last resort I could break the window, but that would make a lot of noise. Mrs. Abington would be sure to wake up and come to see. And if she did that for *any* reason . . . well, I had the heavy hammer, and I would . . . I would do whatever I had to do. One way or another, Sam and I were getting away from her before the night ended.

It took forever to pull a nail out of the second board. It was a huge nail, almost more than I was equal to. The thing moved only the tiniest fraction at a time, and my shirt was wet with perspiration before I had finished. I had to be so careful; at the least suggestion of noise, I'd have to stop and wait and listen. But finally the nail came free. Then I had to begin on the last one.

It might have been a little easier, or perhaps it just seemed that way because I was so close to freedom by then. Even Sam appeared to be feeling my impatience and anxiety; he fidgeted and moved around in his sleep, and I made him a silent promise: If I could only get us free, I would get back to where we'd started from in the quickest possible time, and I would never again take a stupid risk that could harm another soul!

I thought of Robert Burns's poem that we'd read in English II, the one about the field mouse whose "house" was destroyed by the farm worker with his plow. The point to the poem was that even our most carefully prepared plans can be turned upside down without a second's warning, and I thought that Sam and I were like the poor little mouse. My "plans" hadn't been well prepared at all, but it seemed that *everything* I'd done since the seventeeth of August had gone upside down and inside out. Such thoughts weren't too encouraging as I finally began to get somewhere with the last nail. Would this effort, like the other choices I'd made lately, go astray?

The claws of the hammer slipped off the board twice. The first time, with all my weight against the hammer when it gave way, I staggered backward across the floor, barely keeping myself upright. I was more careful as I began tugging and gasping once more.

Then it came loose, and I practically dived for the board to keep it from hitting the floor with a bang. Somehow I did it, with a long sliver of wood in my hand for my efforts.

I laid the board aside gently, then, gritting my teeth, I pulled the big splinter out of my hand. It hurt. Just remembering it, I have to clench my teeth and I shiver all over.

Then I was at the window again, sliding my hand under the next board and up, until I touched the latch holding the window tightly closed. At first it wouldn't budge. It had been fastened tightly for a very long time, and there wasn't much space for my fingers to work. I began to fear that I would have to take off yet another board, but finally the latch gave way and opened. I breathed a deep sigh of relief. I had done it! Sam and I were all but free!

I opened the window, and it stayed in place. Quickly then I grabbed up my backpack, extended it through the window, and dropped it. Thankfully, it made no sound. Then I slipped my arms around Sam and lifted him. He wiggled restlessly, then settled into my arms. I stooped with him, bent my knees, and stuck one leg through the window, precariously balanced.

The door opened.

I froze in place. I had left the light on, and there she stood in the doorway with an expression of bug-eyed surprise on her face and a gleaming butcher knife in her hand. She recovered quickly, drawing in her breath with a sharp sound. Then she said, "Get back in here!"

With painful slowness I drew my leg back inside, my mind going frantically. I was so close—so very close, but I *couldn't* jump out. I didn't know what was on the ground outside the window, and I had Sam in my arms. I wanted to jump anyway, rather than to come back inside with her and that horrible knife, but the hammer was right there on the bed, just a foot or so from my hand. At least I had a weapon, too, unless she saw it first.

"Put him on the bed," she growled at me. "Are you crazy, climbing out the window like that? You could hurt him!"

Slowly I moved against the bed, laying Sam down, with my eyes on the wicked-looking knife. It was a foot long or more, with a wide, sharp blade. A very efficient sort of knife. Was it the same one she had used to slaughter her husband and her son?

My stomach churned, but my left hand closed around the handle of the hammer, and I straightened, slipping that hand behind me. I would try to get just a little closer, and then . . .

Bang! Bang! Bang!

I froze at the unexpected pounding on the back door, but Mrs. Abington's eyes widened in absolute terror. The fear on her face was a remarkable thing to see, and she appeared to shrink before my eyes, as she cringed against the wall.

The pounding came again, then a voice. "Open up, Jane," a man's voice called out in a pleasant, friendly tone. "It's Sheriff Ritter. Come on now Jane, open the door. You know you've got no reason to be afraid of me!"

Jane Abington did not or could not answer. She seemed not to have even heard the sheriff's words, for she remained scrunched against the wall as though trying to press herself into it. The knife was still clenched in her hand, though I felt sure by then that she was no longer really aware of it.

Slowly I approached her, but I still held my own weapon; there was no way of knowing what she might do. My heart pounded and I couldn't pull the air deeply enough into my lungs.

"Mrs. Abington," I began tentatively, "put the knife on the floor, won't you please?"

She did not respond, and I tried again. "The man outside—the sheriff—he sounded like a friend. Is he a friend of yours, Mrs. Abington? He said you have no reason to be afraid of him. Why don't you put the knife down and open the door?"

The pounding at the back door sounded again, and again the voice called out, "Open the door, Jane! I'm here to help you. Don't be afraid; let me in."

Still she made no response. She seemed paralyzed, and I thought I could probably take a couple more steps and simply take the knife out of her hand. But I was afraid. I was dimly aware that Sam had awakened, and that scared me more. I was afraid for his safety and also afraid of what he might see during the next few minutes.

"Ma'Lou!" he called plaintively, but I couldn't answer him. I didn't even turn around, for I did not want to turn my back on the woman. Again Sam called my name, and again, louder than before.

Then when he still received no recognition, he yelled out his next attempt: "D'ane Abington!"

I could not believe my own eyes. She began to relax visi-

116

bly. Her shoulders loosened, and she gradually stood more erect as her eyes moved, finally settling on Sam. Then she glanced at her own hand clenched around the knife handle, and slowly, slowly, she reached it out toward me. I couldn't move a muscle.

"Take it," she said in a harsh, guttural voice.

I reached out and took the knife, and she moved, standing her full height at last. Still moving in a strange kind of slow motion, she left the room and went to the kitchen door and unlocked it, then backed away to stand motionless, her arms hanging loosely.

Immediately a hefty gray-haired man in uniform entered the dimly lighted kitchen. He looked into the bedroom and glanced toward me, still holding the knife and the hammer, and he came and gently took them from me. Then he looked around at Sam, nodding his head.

"Everything's fine," he called out. "Come on in here, boy." Then came the biggest surprise of all. He put the knife and the hammer on the kitchen table, then stepped close to Mrs. Abington and enfolded her in his muscular arms.

"It's all right now, Jane," he said softly, holding her. "Nobody's going to hurt you, I promise."

Chapter Seventeen

I FELT AS though I'd been standing in the same spot for hours, but I was so weak I was afraid to move. So I simply stood there watching the amazing—and confusing—warmth and tenderness with which the sheriff treated Mrs. Abington.

Then suddenly Danny appeared beside me, and when he wrapped his arms around me, I burst into tears, to my own surprise. A moment later we were seated on the bed, and Danny was holding me while Sam climbed all over both of us, saying, "Dan-nee, Dan-nee," and patting Danny's face, then mine.

In a little while I recovered from the tears and the weakness and the trembling and terror. The sheriff had taken Mrs. Abington into her bedroom. I could hear him talking gently to her, and the sound of dresser drawers being opened and closed.

When I wondered aloud to Danny about what was happening, he said the sheriff was taking Mrs. Abington to a hospital.

"A hospital?" I asked, amazed. "To prison would make more sense. She kidnapped us, Danny!" The sound of the word I had used bothered me, but I went on. "It's even worse than that," I said. "She's already been in prison, Danny, for killing her own husband and son!"

"Sh-h-h-h," Danny whispered. "She didn't kill anyone, Marylou."

"But I read the newspaper clippings," I protested. "They're right there in that dresser drawer!"

"I don't know about that," Danny said, "though the sheriff told me about how she was convicted and then released later. He also said that he had known Mrs. Abington all her life, and that he kept the investigation into the killings going. And after she was acquitted at the second trial, he found the real killer, and he's in the state penitentiary now—and for the rest of his life."

"But what . . . she kept us here, Danny, and the knife . . . you saw the knife. She was going to . . ."

"Just protect you and Sam, would be my guess, after the things the sheriff told me," Danny said softly. "She probably heard something and thought it was an intruder. The sheriff said Mrs. Abington couldn't hurt a fly, but that since that awful tragedy, she's been petrified, afraid of people, afraid of going out of the house. . . ."

"Even afraid of light," I murmured as I began to understand a little. Then, "Danny, how did you know Sam and I were here?"

He shook his head and grinned, appearing embarrassed. "I don't understand it myself," he said shyly. "I guess I just sort of—felt it at first. When I came out and found that you and Sam were gone, I was pretty disappointed. But then I . . . I found that piece of paper that I'd given you."

"With your address on it," I murmured.

"Yeah. And for a moment I was mad, or . . . or hurt, I guess. That you'd left it behind. But I just couldn't really *believe* that you'd have done that on purpose. So after work that night, I came back out here. I prowled around outside the house, and I had the strongest feeling that you and Sam were here. I couldn't shake that feeling, but I was afraid to just come and knock on the door and ask, for some reason. So I came back the second night too, and I saw all the water on the ground by the pump, so I knew *somebody* was here. So then I asked my boss about this place, and he said some kind of crazy hermit woman lived here, but he didn't know anything else. Anyway, I just . . . kept coming back. And tonight, when I found the note you left outside, when I saw it was that address you'd written on it, I knew something was seriously wrong. So I went back to town and got the sheriff.''

He hesitated for a moment. "But Marylou . . . I did have to tell the sheriff about . . . you know, about you and Sam. He had to know why you were out here to start with, and all that. So I had to tell him.''

"That's all right, Danny," I assured him. "I'm just so glad—so glad I can't begin to tell you. I've been scared to death! I wish I could understand why she kept us here like she did!''

"Probably she was just so awful lonesome," he said, "but who can tell? According to the sheriff, she's been getting worse and worse lately. He said he's been trying to kind of keep an eye on her, and he's been worried.''

All of us rode back into Swifton in the sheriff's car. It was a sad, silent few minutes. He turned us over to the other people at his office, then he went on, somewhere, with Mrs. Abington.

It was a long and terrible night, altogether. Before it was over, Sam and I were on our way back down the highway I'd walked away from home on, the night I ran away on the seventeenth of August.

It took a long time to get there, but not long enough for me, because I knew they'd take Sam away from me as soon as we arrived. I held him in my arms almost all the way, while he slept peacefully. I wished that he could be awake during our last couple of hours together, yet I was glad too that he was so peaceful. I tried to keep my eyes dry and my mind clear, so I would be able to remember the warmth and sweetness of him forever.

There's no point in going into all the painful details, but it amounted to this: When we finally reached that ugly little town where I'd grown up, we drove past Uncle Ed's house and directly to that county sheriff's office. Mr. Patterson and a lady social worker were there, and they took Sam right out

120

of my arms. They refused to tell me where they were taking him.

Then after a few official odds and ends that I truly don't remember very well—because it was all I could do to control myself and not go to pieces from the hurt of losing Sam—I was driven to a big house, some kind of "home," somebody said, and a man in a wheelchair met us at the door. Then his wife was there, and I wasn't actually seeing or hearing much of anything, but she was kind, and she took me to a clean, comfortable bedroom where I fell asleep. I stayed asleep for a long, long time.

Chapter Eighteen

I STAYED IN that home—the parents were Mr. and Mrs. Burns—for almost two weeks before I had to go to court. Those days were physically comfortable because it was such a nice family and they were always good to me. Nobody put me down or gave me a hard time about the wrong things I'd done, and I felt grateful for that. I tried to make myself useful there, and that was easy enough. In a big house with a big family, there's always plenty of work to do. Of course everybody there did his part, but I felt like I owed a lot extra, not just to that family, but to . . . well, to the whole world, almost. The work kept me occupied, but it was more to me than that. It was my way of apologizing to the good and responsible people of the world for the mistakes I'd made.

I didn't ask any questions because the only thing that really mattered very much was Sam, and I'd already lost him. It left a great big hollow place inside me that hurt more than I could ever explain. I didn't exactly become accustomed to it, although I spent most of my thoughts in trying to make myself believe that Sam would be all right. I tried to convince myself that even if he'd been taken back to Uncle Ed and Aunt Bonnie, they wouldn't dare do anything to hurt him after everything that had happened. I tried very hard to believe that at least he was in the care of adults, whoever they were, and that he was probably better off because of that.

On the evening before I was to go to court, I wasn't even nervous. It wasn't that I didn't care what would happen. I cared a lot. I expected to be sent to reform school and I surely didn't want to go there; scenes from the previous winter's visit there kept popping into my mind, and they certainly weren't pleasant.

But in a way, it was a relief to have it all out of my hands, so to speak. I had no decisions to make and no problems to solve. I had lost the right to make choices, and though I knew in my head that I would eventually hate that, for the present it wasn't bad at all. I didn't even choose what the cook would fix me for breakfast, which was an option we all had in that home. The woman who did the cooking was the only hired help, and whatever she fixed, I ate. She was a warm, grandmotherly sort of woman, and I liked her a lot, too. At breakfast on the morning I was to go to court, she asked me a curious question.

"If the judge should say that you could live here until you're of age, what would you say to that?" she asked me.

"I'd love it of course," I replied instantly. "Who wouldn't want to live here? But there's no chance of that, not after the mess I made of things."

She smiled and gave me a quick hug. "I don't expect you'll be treated like a hardened criminal, honey," she replied. "If I was the judge, I'd say this is the perfect place for you to live."

I appreciated her feelings and her goodness in trying to lift my spirits. It *would* be lovely to really live in such a home, I thought. It certainly wasn't anything like living with Uncle Ed and Aunt Bonnie, but being told I could stay there would be more of a reward than a punishment, and there was no point in even thinking about such an impossibility.

The sheriff's deputy, Randy Stone, came to pick me up. The Burnses would be in court, too, they had told me, but I had to get there early for a private "conversation" with the judge before the actual official court business.

I dreaded it. I imagined a stern old man with bifocals over frightful, piercing eyes, and hair the color of a stormy day in summer. He would be objective and unbending, sticking to the letter of the law and dispensing rigid justice to all those who had failed to honor the law. . . .

Deputy Stone took me to a solid wood door halfway down a dreary hall in the courthouse, and knocked. Someone said, "Come in," and Randy opened the door for me.

"Good luck Marylou," he whispered as I started through the door. I tried to smile, but I'm not sure it came off just right.

The judge's office felt homey and comfortable. It was lighted by several attractive lamps, and the ancient wood furnishings gleamed warmly. Behind an enormous desk sat a pretty woman of thirty-five or so. She had black hair and a soft olive complexion, and smiling brown eyes. I figured she must be the judge's secretary, but I was wrong.

"So you're Marylou Britten," she said pleasantly. "I'm Judge Carmen Silva. Have a seat, Marylou. Let's get acquainted."

My surprise must have been showing, for she wore a teasing grin when I mumbled some kind of greeting. But then she got right down to business. She started by asking me how I felt about school and about education in general, and then she asked a lot of questions about my childhood. They were simple things she wanted to know, such as what kinds of toys I had enjoyed most as a child, about things like bedtime rituals and whether I'd been afraid of the dark or whether I had enjoyed fairy tales, or watched television a lot.

Then she asked a few simple things about Uncle Ed and Aunt Bonnie, and finally, about Sam and me. Until she got to that, I didn't have any trouble, but it was pretty hard for me to talk about Sam. I kept getting choked up, but she was patient and I got through it.

She said I should tell her about the stuff that happened after I ran away with Sam, and every now and then she'd interrupt with a question. She asked why I had left the house where Danny and the other kids lived, and I tried to explain. Then she wanted to know why I hadn't just hit Mrs. Abington over the head with something and got away from there the first day.

That was a tough one and I had to think about it. Finally I said, "I didn't want to hurt her even though I was really scared when she acted so weird. She seemed so—like the whole world had deserted her or something, and mad as I was, I guess I felt sorry for her, too. But I *would* have done something like that eventually I guess. Or any time, if she hadn't been good to Sam. But she did try to be good to him. She made him all those toys I told you about, and she always fixed him an egg. He sort of liked her."

The judge nodded, without comment. Then she asked me about the past week and a half, how it had been, living with the Burns's, and I told her the truth: that sometimes it seemed a little noisy and crowded in the evenings, but that it was still the best, friendliest, kindest home I'd ever imagined.

That seemed to be about it. I couldn't tell anything about what she was thinking or even begin to guess what she had in mind for me. I really wanted to ask what had happened to Sam, and finally I got up the nerve.

"Do you mean that Mr. Patterson didn't tell you?" she asked, surprised.

"No," I said. "I begged him to tell me where they were taking him, but he said it wasn't my place to know."

The judge frowned. "That seems to have been . . . unnecessary," she said. I thought she wanted to say more, but she didn't.

"Sam is well and happy," she said. "He's in the temporary care of a young couple right here in town, and they have a little boy right near Sam's age. You should see those two; they have a great time together. I went to visit them myself yesterday, and I can assure you that Sam is just fine."

Then she picked up a manila envelope from her desk. "I'm going to ask that you forgive me for reading this," she said. "It's your mail; it was brought here to my office just this morning, and I thought that if I could know something more about you . . . well, it had already been opened, and I read it. You should read it now, I think."

The envelope was from an editor at *Seventeen* magazine, and I saw first of all that they had returned my story. I wasn't surprised, but my stomach did kind of ache a little. Even through all the stuff that had happened since I'd run away, I had thought about that story quite a lot. I had realized several things that weren't quite right about it, but to tell the whole truth, I'd still thought it was pretty good. But they'd sent it back.

I guess I was just sitting there holding it, because the judge said, "Read the letter, Marylou."

So I did. The first two sentences were something like, "Thank you for submitting your story to us. Unfortunately, in its present form, it doesn't quite suit our needs."

But then the editor went on to say that the weaknesses in the story could be corrected, and there were several suggestions about how I could do that, and they really did make sense to me. And then, wonder of wonders, "If you would like to revise your story along these lines, we would be very interested in giving it another reading."

I couldn't believe I'd read it correctly at first. I reread that last sentence several times, and it thrilled me with a kind of joy that I had never experienced before. It was as if someone was telling me for the first time in my life that I had some value, that I was *worth* something in this world. Surely, I thought, very little else could ever bring me such pure joy, such happiness!

Then I realized something else that letter meant, and I started to cry. I knew the judge was watching me, but I just couldn't help it. She let me cry for a minute, and then she said, "Why the tears, Marylou? It seems to me that letter should make you a very happy girl. Why, it's more than any beginning writer, especially at your age, could expect, isn't it?"

"That's just it," I finally managed to say. "It *is* wonderful, almost too wonderful to believe. But I . . . look at all the stuff I've done. I thought everything was hopeless. But it wasn't hopeless at all. I actually had a chance, and now I've messed everything up. I've ruined . . . everything!"

"Oh, I wouldn't say that, Marylou," the judge murmured. "I don't think things are quite that bad. The Burnses should be here by now, and our friend Mr. Patterson. Let me call them in here, and we'll see what's to be done about you.''

In a few moments the judge's office was filled to the brim. I had sort of expected Uncle Ed and Aunt Bonnie to be there, but they weren't.

The whole thing didn't take as long as I had thought it would. It was sort of informal, although Judge Silva was unquestionably in control of the whole proceeding. First she asked questions of Mr. Patterson. It seemed to me that he was more concerned with convincing the judge that he hadn't been at fault than anything else. But maybe I'm wrong about that. Sometimes it's pretty hard to be completely fair with someone you don't like.

Then she talked to Mr. and Mrs. Burns, and they said they would like to have me live with them. That brought more tears to my eyes, but I managed not to cry outright. It was awfully kind of them to try to save me like that.

There were only two mentions of reform school. Mr. Patterson mentioned it as ''one of our options,'' but I thought the judge didn't seem too enthusiastic about it. Anyway, after a while the judge made her decision.

''Marylou Britten, it is the opinion of this court that the most appropriate disposition is for you to remain under the guardianship of Mr. and Mrs. Burns until you come of age.''

All the Christmases in the world combined couldn't touch that single gift. I don't know a better way to say it. When I tried to thank the judge, she said, ''Just finish your growing up, Marylou. I have the deepest confidence that you will make a fine contribution to society one day. To prevent that from becoming a reality by sending you to a correctional facility seems to be the most foolish and wasteful choice I could possibly make.''

She had several more things to say, especially to me, and when she was finished, she asked me to wait outside. She had further business with Mr. and Mrs. Burns and Mr. Patterson, she said.

While I waited, I thought about how fortunate I was, about

127

what it would be like to be a member of the Burns's big family while I finished school . . . and about Sam.

If only I hadn't lost Sam, everything would be completely perfect. But I had known it would happen, and I had already been given much, much more than I'd had any right to expect. If only I could know that my precious little Sam would have as good a life as the judge had given me!

In a little while Mr. and Mrs. Burns came out, and they both hugged me and told me they were glad that I would be a part of their family from then on. It was the most wonderful, the most beautiful . . . it was *almost* completely perfect.

Chapter Nineteen

FOR SEVERAL WEEKS after court was over, I kept thinking about how I might have hurt Sam. When I think about how close it was, about all the terrible things that could have happened, well, it makes me break out in goose bumps all over.

Now I know the things I *should* have done. To begin with, I should have made such a fuss with Mr. Patterson that he would've *had* to listen. Failing that, I could have talked to someone else; *someone* would have listened. To have given up after the first failure to get someone's attention for Sam . . . I can hardly believe I did that. I mean, in my right mind I'm not stupid. Of course I *wasn't* in my right mind on the seventeenth of August, and that brings me to the next "should have." I should have asked someone to help *me*, instead of running away.

There are a lot more such things I should have done and not done, and they're probably all pretty obvious to anyone who knows the whole story. I won't forget those awful mistakes I made, not ever.

But the wonderful thing (and it's more than I deserve, but I'm not turning it down!) is that I don't have to keep thinking of my mistakes all the time, not anymore. I wish I had the words to say just how marvelous it feels not to be weighted down with worries and troubles every minute, but it's beyond description. The closest I can come to saying it is that it's kind of like fifty percent of the effects of gravity have been suspended, just for me. I feel so *light* nowadays. I feel *free*, and I also feel, for the first time ever I think, like a teenager.

And yet, maybe I'll always be a little "older" than other people my age in some ways, and maybe that's not bad. Maybe after all that's happened, I will have sense enough to always appreciate the truly good people in the world, like the truck driver, and like some others I'll be describing in a moment.

I hope I will not forget to be tolerant and compassionate with people who are sick, like Mrs. Abington. She's in a hospital now, being treated for photophobia, agoraphobia, and severe depression. Most everybody knows what depression is; photophobia is not being able to tolerate light, and agoraphobia, at least in Mrs. Abington's case, is being afraid to leave her house. They say it's all curable. I hope so. It was a scary time that Sam and I spent with her, but she really wasn't a witch. She meant no harm; she was just so terribly lonesome and afraid of people. It must have been unbelievably miserable for her, and it would be nice to learn sometime that she's happy and healthy again.

What I hope for most I think, for myself I mean, is that I can someday have the wisdom to understand people better, and to really know how to be . . . whatever I need to be with people. I said that very thing to Mr. Burns yesterday, and he said, "Well, Marylou, I'm forty-five, and *I'm* still waiting for that kind of wisdom, but let's not give up."

Mr. Burns and his wife Martha are some terribly important people in my life now. Sam is first of course, and then there's Danny. But Mr. and Mrs. Burns are super-special too.

They are the kind of parents every kid ought to have. And speaking of kids, they're *everywhere*. The Burnses have adopted some and are foster parents to others, and I don't know which are which. There are nine of us kids altogether, and we live in this house that's so big that you could get lost in it. It's not fancy, just big and kind of sprawled out, but we do have three full bathrooms. There are six big old oak trees in the yard, and swings, and tree houses, and twenty acres, so I can always go for a safe walk when I need a little time to myself.

After growing up so all alone, it does seem pretty crowded and noisy around here sometimes, and I'll tell the truth . . . now and then it gets on my nerves. That's when I go out for a walk, and it's nice and restful, but the neat thing is that I'm always glad to get back! You see, I didn't know there was so much love in the whole world as there is right here in this house. Mrs. Burns says it's simple, that the more love you give, the more you *have* to give, and it won't run out unless you stop loving.

Don't misunderstand; it's not all hugs and kisses around here. The kids have squabbles all the time over who has borrowed whose clothes or whose turn it is to rake the leaves or do the laundry. But those squabbles don't have much to do with anger, and they pass quickly. If they occasionally don't, Mr. Burns manages to settle things with just a few gentle words. That's one of his "jobs," he says.

He looks a lot like the television character, Ben Cartwright, and he's here about all the time. He doesn't go out to a job to work, but he's always busy just the same. He can do about anything, and that's pretty remarkable because he's in a wheelchair. Mr. Burns was wounded in Vietnam.

That's sad of course, but as he says, it's the way things *are*, so there's no future in crying about it. Besides, he says, there's an advantage in being in a wheelchair: he gets to spend a lot of time with one kid or another on his lap.

Sam spends a lot of time there.

Yes, I saved the best part for the last. The judge let the Burnses take Sam, too, and they're in the process of adopting him. That makes me very happy. It was strange, I thought, that the judge cautioned *me*. What she said was, "Marylou, in spite of your mistakes, you've tried to do what you thought was right for Sam, and we all know that you love him. But now you're going to have to start thinking a little differently about him. Mr. and Mrs. Burns will be his parents now, and you're going to have to trust their judgment and abide by their decisions where Sam is concerned."

I thought that was a silly kind of caution. Wasn't that just what I had wanted for Sam, a good home and family where he would be cared for and loved? But the judge knew what she was doing, because there were several times when I had to bite my tongue, like when the other kids here played a little too roughly with him or when Sam had to learn the hard way that he'd have to share his toys and attention with the others from now on. At those times Mr. and Mrs. Burns were kind to me, but firm. "He has to learn to live in a big family now, Marylou," they'd tell me. "If things come out a bit unequally for any of you here, it's more than made up for in all the love we have for one another, isn't it?" And of course they're right.

I still take care of Sam a lot, and he still runs to me when he gets a bump or gets his feelings hurt—most of the time anyway. He has learned, though, that it doesn't *have* to be me who kisses his hurts or plays with him, and if I still feel a little twinge of jealousy now and then when he turns to someone else, well, that's normal enough. I'm certain that I'll never love Sam any less, but in my head I know that it's better for him not to be depending completely on me for everything. Besides, he's the baby of the family here. He surely doesn't lack for attention!

I'm going to a different school now, and I really like it. I even have a great English teacher who's interested in my writing and helps me a lot. She's not Miss Worth, but she's kind and helpful, and she is even a writer herself, so she really knows how to advise me. I've revised my story like the *Seventeen* editor suggested, and I put it in the mail again yesterday. I really think they will accept it and publish it this time, but even if they don't, I'll keep writing until I *do* get published. At least I know now that it's *possible* for me to become a real writer.

Speaking of writing, Danny and I exchange letters often. He's still working, and living in the little house. He tells me he has become friends with a couple of the guys who work with him, and that they have even persuaded him to go back to school, because that's what they're doing. Not regular school of course, but the three of them are going to GED classes, and before too long, Danny will take the test to get his high school equivalency diploma. I asked him in a letter if he thought that would be the end of his education or not, and he said that he hadn't thought about it much yet, but that he was enjoying the GED classes, much to his surprise.

Danny has already come here to the Burns's to visit me once, and he's coming again in about a month. I don't know what will happen in the future between Danny and me, and I don't think too much about that, either. It's good the way it is now. Danny and I are the best of friends, and both of us put an awful lot of value on that friendship. We'll tackle the future a day at a time and try to be grateful that, at last, we *can* look at it that way.

There's just one more thing that I need to say, and it concerns something that's been really difficult for me.

I'd been so bitter about Uncle Ed and Aunt Bonnie, and I hated having those ugly feelings inside me, but I couldn't get them to go away. Then one day Mr. Burns said, ''What's wrong, Marylou? Why so sad?''

I suppose he just happened to catch me at the wrong moment, or maybe the right one, because I started bawling. ''Why couldn't they have loved Sam and me?'' I asked. ''What's so difficult about that? Everything would have been fine if they just could have loved us a little!''

Mr. Burns didn't have any answer to that, but he did have a suggestion. ''You can't make other people feel the way you want them to feel, Marylou,'' he said, ''so what you've got to do is to change your own feelings about *them*.''

''Why should I?'' I asked, ''even if I could, I mean.''

''Oh, you can,'' he replied with a gentle smile, ''and you must. Why? Because when you're bitter about something, the bitterness is like a poison that seeps all through you. It weakens your character a little bit at a time, and the result is that you can't make the best of yourself. You're old enough to know that's true.''

''Supposing you're right,'' I said, ''how would I go about

changing my feelings about Uncle Ed and Aunt Bonnie? It doesn't seem possible."

His answer was the most ridiculous thing I'd ever heard in my life!

"Write them a letter, telling them exactly how you feel about them," he said.

"I thought you were going to say I should forgive them," I said. "What good would such a letter do? It would only hurt their feelings, if they have any feelings about me, and it would probably wind up making me feel ashamed."

"Oh, you mustn't *mail* the letter," Mr. Burns said. "Just write it, and then you tear it up. Then wait a day or so and do it again, and tear that one up. Then you write another one, and so on, until you finally come up with a letter that you really want to mail. It'll take awhile, maybe a *lot* of tries, but I think you'll find that the result will be just what you need."

His suggestion was so weird that I didn't even try it for about a week, but since I couldn't get them off my mind, I finally decided, what the heck, might as well give it a whirl.

That first letter was so mean and nasty even I couldn't believe it. I hadn't known I had so much meanness in me. Then I wrote another one the next day, after I tore the first one up, and guess what: it wasn't quite so vicious. Well, I wrote Uncle Ed and Aunt Bonnie a total of thirteen letters, believe it or not, and when I finished the thirteenth letter, I asked Mr. Burns to read it.

He did, and he sat thinking it over for a while, then he said, "This is the way you really, truly feel?"

I said it was.

"Then mail it," he said.

This is a copy of the letter I wrote.

Dear Uncle Ed and Aunt Bonnie,

I hope you are both feeling good and that things are going well for you. Sam and I are very happy here. Sam has lots of people to love him, and so do I. He's getting cuter and sweeter and smarter every day I think. He will have a good childhood here with Mr. and Mrs. Burns and a houseful of brothers and sisters.

I am enjoying school and keeping my grades up, and I want to thank you for always making me study and do my homework when I was little. That got me started out right in school. I still plan to go to college after I graduate.

I remember some nice things from when I was little, and I think about those things a lot, lately. Thank you for taking me in and raising me. I'm sorry for the worry I must have caused you.

If you would like for me to visit you, write and let me know. Mr. Burns has already told me that he'll be happy to bring me, but if you'd rather that I didn't come, I will understand.

Please take care of yourselves, and please try to keep a few nice memories. I hope to see you soon.

With love, from Sam and me.

About the Author

Nadine Roberts is a teacher of high school English in Naylor, Missouri. Ms. Roberts has also written handbooks on taxidermy and stone masonry. Married with three children and six grandchildren, Ms. Roberts nevertheless finds time for boating and camping.

*Useful Advice
For Young Adults
As Only
Hila Colman
Can Give*